VE APR 8

009835

Where the
Fraser River
Flows

Where the Fraser River Flows

The Industrial Workers of the World
in British Columbia

MARK LEIER

1990 New Star Books Vancouver

Printed and bound in Canada
1 2 3 4 5   94 93 92 91 90
First printing July 1990

The publisher is grateful for assistance provided by the Canada Council and the Cultural Services Branch, Province of British Columbia.

New Star Books Ltd.
2504 York Avenue
Vancouver, B.C.
V6K 1E3

Canadian Cataloguing in Publication Data

Leier, James Mark.
  Where the Fraser River flows

  Includes bibliographical references.
  ISBN 0-921586-02-7 (bound). – ISBN 0-921586-01-9 (pbk.)

  1. Industrial Workers of the World – History.   2. Labor and laboring classes – British Columbia – History.   3. Trade-unions – British Columbia – History.   I. Title.
  HD6529.B7L44 1989   331.88'09711   C89-091399-4

To my parents, Jim and Margaret,
and to my brother, Ben.

Contents

Preface

The Industrial Workers of the World has not been treated well by modern historians. This is a surprising claim to make in light of the extensive work on the union published in the last twenty-five years. Several historians, among them Melvyn Dubofsky, Philip Foner, and Joseph Conlin, have examined the IWW in great detail. Its story has been charted from northern British Columbia to Australia, from the founding convention of 1905 to the failures of the 1970s. The histories of Wobbly martyrs have been well documented, and even the IWW's "songs to fan the flames of discontent" are well-known.

Why then another book on the IWW? In spite of the meticulous attention paid to the historical record, the beliefs that inspired the songs and urged on the martyrs have been treated with condescension. Historians have been quick to judge the ideology of the IWW and find it wanting. Nurtured on the Wagner Act and the post-war settlement between labour and capital, most historians view the syndicalism of the Wobblies as quixotic. Liberal historians prefer the parliamentary shadow-boxing of the welfare state and social democracy to the direct action of the IWW, while Marxist-Leninists attack the critique of the vanguard and the state that it posed. Historians friendly to the modern labour movement prefer the class collaboration of the AFL-CIO to the class warfare of the Wobblies. Since the IWW and anarcho-syndicalism were effectively beaten by competing ideologies by the end of the Second World War, most historians assume they must have been truncated lines of evolution. The IWW is often considered quaint but hopelessly utopian and irrelevant to the history of the modern world.

But these assumptions deprive us of many valuable insights. If we set aside the judgement of these historians and see the IWW as a realistic historical alternative, we view the development of class relations in North America from a very different perspective. We gain a new understanding of the specific role of monopoly capitalism in redefining the work process and work relations. We appreciate how different parts of the working class responded to new pressure in different ways; we see how socialist and labour leaders preferred to abandon syndicalism in order to seek compromises with capital and the state. These compromises may have initially benefitted segments of the working class, but ultimately they strengthened the dominance of capital, for they made the trade union movement and social democracy the agents of the reforms necessary to keep the system going. I will attempt to take a new look at the vaunted radicalism of British Columbia through an analysis of the IWW. Using the IWW as a yardstick, it will be easier to see the twists and turns of the labour and socialist movements as they try to reach an accord with capital and the state in the years before World War One.

Many of the following pages deal not with the facts and minutiae of the union, but with the work of other writers. Historians do not just record history: they interpret it, and they bring to it their own views on politics, capitalism, activism, and morality. Even those who claim they have no particular political stance, or that they write only to entertain, must use their own world-view to decide what is important, what is entertaining, and what is interesting. If one believes that Canada is essentially a democratic, prosperous nation with great and equal opportunity for all, one asks different questions and gets different answers than if one believes that there is a ruling class with privilege and power. If one believes the working class smells, one writes differently than if one believes it is heroic. This is as true in studying the IWW as any other part of society. The book is an attempt to compensate for the liberal and social democractic histories that are too quick to write off the IWW; it tries to treat syndicalism as a powerful and plausible alternative to capitalism and state socialism. By doing so, it sheds light on working-class solidarity and fragmentation in the B.C. labour movement before the First World War.

A few notes on the organization of this book. I am aware that long quotations and footnotes are often considered tedious. Despite this, I have quoted extensively from the radical press. I have done so in order to preserve the punch of the IWW's ideology and to let Wobblies speak for themselves. Since I argue with some historians, it is necessary to use their words, and to footnote them, to avoid charges of quoting out of context or of misrepresentation. It is my hope that footnotes will aid the more skeptical reader as well as the one who wishes to find out more about a topic. Footnotes also acknowledge some of the debts I have to the work of others. Finally, they are used to discuss ideas and arguments that will be, to many readers, of the "How many Hegels can dance on the head of a pin?" variety. The fuller history of the word "Wobbly," for example, and discussions on syndicalism and direct action, have been moved out of the main text. It is hoped that as footnotes these items will provide more information to those who are interested and be out of the way of those who are not.

A large part of this book was originally written as a master's thesis at Simon Fraser University. Allen Seager, as supervisor, and Don Kirschner, as a committee of one, oversaw the work, and I am grateful for their advice and criticism. Bryan D. Palmer and John H. Thompson read my early work on the IWW and urged me to continue my research, while Greg Kealey encouraged me to turn the thesis into a book. Though they represent a number of different political and historical traditions, these professors have given generously of their time and knowledge.

It is often said that graduate students learn as much from each other as they do from their professors. In this light, it is appropriate to thank especially Craig Derksen, Wendie Nelson, and Randy Wick. I would also like to thank Sean Cadigan of Memorial University for his uncanny ability to disagree with nearly everything I say and for his warm friendship.

Al Grierson and Mark Warrior were the first Wobblies I met. We have worked, debated, and marched together for some years now, and I continue to draw upon their expertise in folklore and labour history.

Joanna Koczwarski and Meg Stainsby used their knowledge of modern technology to meet impossible deadlines. They did so with considerable grace under pressure, and without their labour neither the thesis nor the book could have been completed on time.

Portions of Chapters 3 and 4 have appeared in *Labour/Le Travail*, which has graciously allowed me to reprint the material here. Additional research was funded by the Social Science and Humanities Research Council of Canada.

Finally, I wish to thank Annette DeFaveri for her constant support. Quite simply, I could not have done it without her.

CHAPTER 1

Monopoly Capitalism
and the Rise of Syndicalism

By the last years of the nineteenth century, many American and Canadian workers were keenly aware that the craft unions affiliated to the American Federation of Labor and the Trades and Labor Congress of Canada would not alter the basic relations between capital and labour. Unions could continue to carve out better wages for their members, but they would not help the mass of workers who were not organized. Nor would they work to abolish the unjust system of capitalism. At the same time, the socialist movement was isolated from the working class and its daily struggles. Prompted by the Western Federation of Miners and the left wing of the Socialist Party of America, unionists and radicals tried to create a new organization that would be able to unite all workers and work towards revolution as the only way to solve labour's problems once and for all. Late in 1904, workers from the American Labor Union, the United Railway Workers, the Amalgamated Society of Engineers, and the Brewery Workers met to begin the formation of "a labor organization that would correspond to modern industrial conditions." In January 1905, several delegates drew up a manifesto which would lay the foundation for a revolutionary industrial union. The manifesto decried the power of monopoly capitalism and outlined the fundamental changes in the labour process which accompanied it. As machines replaced skilled workers, the tradesman was "sunk in the uniform mass of wage slaves.... Laborers are no longer classified by differences in trade skill, but the employer assorts them according to the machines to which they are attached." Trade unions could not address this problem; at best, they could offer "only a perpetual struggle for slight relief within wage slavery." The manifesto ended with a call for unionists and radicals to assemble in Chicago that June to create a new labour organization.[1]

By early morning on 27 June 1905, Brand's Hall in Chicago

was filled with tobacco smoke and people. More than two hundred delegates had shown up in response to the January manifesto.

The platform attracted most of the famous radicals of the era. Eugene Debs of the Socialist Party of America, Daniel DeLeon of the Socialist Labor Party, Thomas Hagerty, Mother Jones, and Lucy Parsons were all in attendance. Four Canadians had also made their way to Chicago: R.J. Kerrigan and W.F. Leach from Montreal, John Riordan and James Baker from the mining districts of British Columbia.[2]

At 10 a.m., William Dudley Haywood, secretary of the Western Federation of Miners, picked up a short board and pounded this makeshift gavel to silence the crowd. He chose his opening salutation with care, for this new organization did not want to be tainted by rituals and reminders of other radical groups. Haywood wanted to avoid the "brothers and sisters" so redolent of the American Federation of Labor, while "fellow citizens," the address of the French Communards, hardly fit the multilingual and multinational gathering. He brushed aside the "comrades" that had been appropriated by the Socialist Party, and decided on his opening:

> Fellow workers!. . . This is the Continental Congress of the working class. We are here to confederate the workers of this country into a working class movement that shall have for its purpose the emancipation of the working class from the slave bondage of capitalism. There is no organization, or there seems to be no labor organization, that has for its purpose the same object as that for which you are called together today. The aims and objects of this organization should be to put the working class in possession of the economic power, the means of life, in control of the machinery of production and distribution, without regard to capitalist masters.[3]

With this speech the Industrial Workers of the World came into being. It was created to do what the AFL could not, or would not, do: organize unskilled, immigrant workers to fight not just for "more, more, more," but for a revolution that would destroy capitalism and the state.

The radicalism of the IWW was different from that of its

contemporaries, the Socialist Party and the Socialist Labor Party. These parties had come to see the state as the potential liberator of the working class, and believed that the fundamental contradiction of capitalism was its inability to produce and distribute goods fairly and efficiently. Consequently, they believed that the task of the socialists was to take over the state in order to control production and distribution.

The IWW agreed that capitalism was a tyrannical, oppressive way to organize production and distribution. Capitalism meant a handful of people who did little real work reaped the rewards of great wealth, power, and prestige, while those who actually produced society's goods and services were often unable to provide themselves with even basic necessities.

The Wobblies' critique, however, went beyond the socialists' concern for a more equitable distribution of wealth. It was a broader attack on power and privilege as well. Their view, known as syndicalism, held that workers' control was the essential element of socialism, and that the state was as much the enemy as capitalism, for the two were inseparable allies. [4] Most syndicalists would agree with the anarchist Michael Bakunin, who held that the state would always be a tool of oppression, even if it ruled in the name of the workers. Instead of working for a socialist state, the IWW fought for a co-operative commonwealth that would eliminate "such things as the State or States." Rather, worker-controlled "industries will take the place of what are now existing States." One Wobbly's fierce attack on the state socialism of Victor Berger and the Socialist Party of America gives a powerful introduction to the syndicalism of the IWW:

> Berger imagines that Socialism can be attained by a nation operating the industries within its artificial boundaries.... There is no trust nor industry that is confined in one nation, and control of industry, therefore, must finally rest with producers regardless of border lines. In place of "Let the nation own the trusts," it must be "Let the producers control the industries." The first is the slavery of State Socialism; the second is Industrial Freedom....Are we to believe that the State, the mailed fist of the master, based upon exploitation and having as its sole purpose the conserving of property rights...can be of value to the

workers merely by changing its personnel?. . . It is small
consolation to have the State deprive the workers of
industrial liberty in return for the privilege of owning and
managing their own toothbrushes.

Should Berger's ideal become a reality it must of necessity
contain within itself the germ of another revolution. A rebellious working class would rapidly cause such a germ to
mature and burst open State Socialism so as to liberate the
proletariat.

But let us hope we can gain freedom without the necessity
of a second revolution by avoiding the pitfalls of the politicians' dream—State Socialism.

This emphasis on workers' control and local autonomy meant
that the IWW stood for, in the words of a contemporary observer,
a "new kind of revolution"; beside this radicalism, "socialism was
respectable—even reactionary—by comparison."[5]

But if political action—that is, electing left-wing candidates to
capture the state and bring in socialism from above—was reactionary and useless, how was the IWW to make the revolution?
The Wobblies held that the direct action of workers themselves in
the factories and workshops would be able to usher in the new
society. Once the majority of workers were organized in one big
union, they would call a general strike that would paralyze
capitalist society. This would prevent profits, goods, even food,
from going to the capitalists. The workers, who already knew how
to produce and distribute goods, would then take up production
for themselves. As Bill Haywood put it, when the workers were
properly educated and organized, they could "lock the bosses out
and run the factories to suit ourselves."[6]

The IWW did not expect the bosses and the state to surrender
meekly when the general strike broke out. They would fight back
to protect their privilege, and they would use soldiers, machine
guns, and prisons. But if all the workers were organized and united, the armed forces would be useless. Haywood, reflecting on the
Coeur d'Alene strike of 1892, recalled that all the mines were
closed down by the strikers. Mine owners brought in gun thugs,
and the miners fought back with their own weapons. Then mine
owners cried for the government to send militia troops, and they
were sent. But, Haywood asked, "Who brought the soldiers? Railroads manned by union men; engines fired with coal mined by
union men." In a general strike, no trains could roll without the

permission of the workers; no coal would fire the engines; troops would receive neither food, nor shelter, nor munitions.[7]

In the meantime, before the workers were completely organized, the union argued that conditions had to be reformed through industrial action. The IWW fought for higher wages at Lawrence, Massachusetts; for sanitary conditions along the railway camps of the Fraser River; and for shorter hours in Vancouver. But the Wobblies simultaneously insisted that workers must be organized to create a new society in which privilege and want would be unknown. Strikes would make life a little better in the here and now, but they were also

> mere incidents in the class war; they are tests of strength, periodic drills in course of which the workers train themselves for concerted action. This training is most necessary to prepare the masses for the final "catastrophe," the general strike which will complete the expropriation of the employers.[8]

This fusion of revolution and practical labour organizing has led many historians to misinterpret American syndicalism. Joseph Conlin, for example, has gone so far as to argue that the IWW must be seen primarily as a labour union and not as a revolutionary body.[9] Conlin correctly points out that Thomas Hagerty, a founding member of the union who designed its structure, stated that the first function of the organization must be to combine the workers to help them in their struggles for wages and conditions. But Hagerty then argued that the IWW's second function was to "offer a final solution of the labor problem. . . [and] burst the shell of capitalist government and be the agency by which the working people will operate the industries, and appropriate the products to themselves."[10] Conlin suggests also that syndicalism requires the autonomy of industrial unions, and that the IWW was highly centralized. Though the One Big Union structure seems to imply centralization, the rank and file democracy of the IWW meant the union was never centralized. Conlin argues that instead of participatory democracy, syndicalists must adhere to a policy of autonomy for the local union; instead of pledging fealty to the king, members should pledge to the local baron. The IWW held that workers should not be ruled by anyone, a much more democratic and decentralized concept of organization. It is true, as Conlin points out, that Wobblies often

rejected the label of syndicalism, seeing it as a foreign importation. But as Dubofsky points out in his book, the IWW would
reject the label but follow syndicalist policies and actions. Certain
historical differences, such as the pattern of industrialization, and
the dominance and conservatism of Sam Gompers and the AFL,
created organizational and ideological differences, but the IWW
is properly regarded as syndicalist. Conlin seeks to counter earlier
work that saw the IWW merely as an imported revolutionary
aberration, but in playing up the bread and butter side of the
union, he overcorrects. Further, it is making too much of the
Wobblies' practical concern with reform and democracy to argue
that they "evinced a commitment to traditional American liberties." Such a claim obscures the nature of both American liberalism and the syndicalist critique.[11] The IWW was quick to point
out that any resemblance to more conservative unions was only
superficial, and that it did not itself hold with capitalist values:

> The IWW is a revolutionary labor movement, industrial in
> its form, direct in its methods, and open in avowing its
> ultimate purpose of overthrowing the wage system.
>   While better immediate conditions are fought for, they are
> merely incidental to the main object of building an
> organization that will serve to batter on the institutions of
> capitalism and to form the basis of production in the new
> social order.
>   The IWW can never afford to gain in membership at the
> cost of sacrificed principles, or by appealing to the workers
> from the standpoint of immediate material benefits alone.
>   Our outward form may be imperfectly copied by other
> bodies. Our tactics may be applied partially by craft unions
> to gain a higher wage scale. But our spirit of revolt makes us
> stand out from those who acquiesce in the wage system and
> it marks us for the bitter hatred of the employing class. . . .
> The one thing that will keep the IWW from degenerating is
> to foster the spirit of revolt against slavery of any kind.[12]

In his history of the IWW, Philip Foner argues that the union
was too radical. He believes that its opposition to political action
was "a basic error," while the attempt to combine industrial
unionism and revolutionary activity constituted a "fundamental
mistake." Measures that would have ensured the growth and stability of the union were often rejected in favour of revolutionary
principles. For example, the IWW did not sign contracts or have a

dues check-off (the automatic deduction of union dues by the employer). But the refusal to sign contracts allowed employers to regroup and eliminate conditions that had been won once the initial enthusiasm and militancy died away. Renouncing the dues check-off meant the IWW could not generate a stable income, professional leaders, or long-term union membership. The universal transfer system, which made all Wobblies members of any local, tended to give locals a "here today, gone tomorrow" quality, while the refusal to create long-term strike funds hurt the union's endurance in strike actions. Finally, the refusal to provide unemployment and sick benefits meant the IWW could not attract members by supplying specific services.[13]

The IWW did not avoid conventional trade union practice through oversight. Each of these measures, it argued, had a harmful aspect. Signing contracts meant formal acceptance of the employers' legal right to the factory and production, a principle the IWW denied. Contracts limited the right to strike during the agreement, but they did not limit the employers' ability to prepare for strikes through stockpiling, speed-ups, and lay-offs. At the same time, actions by the workers to resist stockpiling and speed-ups, or to hamper production in order to strengthen the union's position, were illegal. The contract was a peace treaty in the class war, but its terms disarmed only the working class.

Collective agreements could even turn the union against its members. In a wildcat strike or job action, the union could be sued and its leaders jailed if they did not order the strikers back to work. In this way, contracts turned the union bureaucracy into policemen for the company. The labour movement could even be pitted against itself, for contracts would force unions to keep working on a site struck by another. Solidarity and militancy would be replaced with acquiescence and placidity, for courts and lawyers would replace the collective action of the workers to enforce conditions and wage rates.[14]

Similarly, the IWW argued that the dues check-off stripped the workers of autonomy and responsibility for their own affairs. As one Wobbly put it, the union "expected grown-up men to be big enough to pay their own dues without a check-off."[15] Automatic check-offs also tended to separate the union from its members, for the job steward was able to avoid the task of going to each worker and collecting complaints and suggestions along with the dues.

The low initiation fees of the IWW did make it difficult to build a war chest, but they also made it possible for unskilled, unemployed, and underpaid workers to join the union. In contrast, the high fees of the AFL often acted as a barrier to workers. Large strike funds could be seized by the state if the union engaged in illegal activity, and workers could not always rely on union officials to issue the money. More importantly, large strike funds encouraged conservatism in the class war, for union leaders were often tempted to keep them intact rather than risk the union's money in a strike. Furthermore, money invested to aid union veterans represented money diverted from the organization and the education needed to bring in new workers; it benefited the "home guard" and labour officials while hurting unionism in the long run. Finally, attracting workers by offering them sick and death benefits did nothing to make them class conscious, or even job conscious. This had the effect of turning working class organizations into "coffin societies," and made the workers collectively responsible for problems caused directly by the employers.[16] The IWW's program resulted from a radical critique of society and the American Federation of Labor. An organizer for the IWW summed up its position concisely:

> Can there be any dispute that if the IWW struck bargains with employers, compromised its principles, signed protocols, contracts, had the employers collect the dues and acted as "good boys" generally, we should have a half million members?...But rather than sacrifice our principles, kowtow to all sorts of freak notions, declare a practical truce with the enemy, and have a large number of duespayers, we have preferred to be true to our own purpose in spite of all opposition. Our men have sweated blood in carrying on the propaganda for a revolutionary labor body—revolutionary in methods as well as final purpose.[17]

Foner's other criticism of the IWW, that industrial unionism was fundamentally incompatible with revolutionary activity, has some truth to it. But this argument is more obvious in the latter part of the twentieth century than it was in the early part. In 1905, the attempt to combine unionism and revolutionary agitation seemed logical and correct. The AFL showed quite clearly what would happen to a union that did not inscribe revolution on its banner. Capitalism would again be accepted and propped up by the workers' organization; huge struggles would be fought, for only slight improvements in conditions, and labour leaders would remain little more than lieutenants for the captains of industry. The basic fact of class conflict would be steadfastly ignored.[18]

On the other side, the Socialist Trade and Labor Alliance showed the futility of creating yet another revolutionary society. The STLA was founded in New York in 1895 to bring a purer, more scientific, and increasingly rarefied version of socialism to the working class. Headed by Daniel DeLeon, a former law professor, the STLA was noted for its rigorous socialist thought and doctrinal purity. It was also noted for its conspicuous inability to attract workers to its fold. Well might DeLeon rail that "you could not first take the men into the union under the false pretense that you were going to raise their wages, and afterward indoctrinate them. No, you had to indoctrinate them first, and then bring them in." Such a policy might have created well-schooled socialists, but it did not create many of them. The STLA never became more than a splinter group, largely because it could offer workers nothing save rhetoric; highly refined rhetoric, to be sure, but still no more substantial.[19]

The IWW effort to combine industrial unionism with revolution made a great deal of sense, for it was an attempt to steer between the Charybdis of opportunism and the Scylla of sectarianism. Yet the failure of the Wobblies cannot be ascribed to this strategy. The Socialist Party advocated and used political action in the way suggested by Foner and came no closer to achieving its goals, while the growing conservatism of the Western Federation of Miners did not save it from extinction after 1905. Both Conlin's attempt to picture the IWW as a conventional trade union and Foner's criticism of its syndicalism block our understanding of the union and the historical conditions that led to it. Their analyses also overlook the fact that the IWW's two-pronged approach— unionism and revolution—was a way out of an old dilemma that often hurt radical groups. Put simply, holding to a pure revolutionary line meant abandoning immediate reforms, for slight improvements would ease the need for revolution; the purist argument held that workers should suffer short-term pain for long-term gain. On the other side, those who were less "pure" argued that such a policy forced worse conditions than were necessary on those living in the present. Further, a pure approach to revolution risked alienating workers who could be won to a program that promised immediate aid and future freedom. In her autobiography, Emma Goldman relates an episode that highlights the dilemma acutely. Sent by Johann Most, the leading American anarchist of the nineteenth century, to agitate against the movement for the eight-hour day in favour of the revolution, she was forced to rethink the position in Cleveland:

> The gist of my talk was the same as in Buffalo, but the form was different. It was a sarcastic arraignment, not of the system or of the capitalist, but of the workers themselves—their readiness to give up a great future for some small temporary gains. . . .
>
> A man in the front row who had attracted my attention by his white hair and lean, haggard face rose to speak. He said that he understood my impatience with such small demands as a few hours less a day, or a few dollars more a week. It was legitimate for young people to take time lightly. But what were men of his age to do? They were not likely to live to see the ultimate overthrow of the capitalist system. Were they also to forgo the release of perhaps two hours a day from the hated work? That was all they could hope to see realized in their lifetime. Should they deny themselves even that small achievement? Should they never have a little more time for reading or being out in the open? Why not be fair to those chained to the block?
>
> The man's earnestness, his clear analysis of the principle involved in the eight-hour struggle, brought home to me the falsity of Most's position. I realized I was committing a crime against myself and the workers by serving as a parrot repeating Most's views. I understood why I had failed to reach my audience.[20]

Combining unionism and revolutionary work, then, made a great deal of tactical sense. Equally important, it illustrates the commitment the IWW had to being a working class organization that represented workers as they were, while educating them to what they could become. Ignoring the day-to-day struggles would set the union apart from its members; the union would become another millenarian scheme, even another boss.

In *We Shall Be All*, Melvyn Dubofsky does attempt to put the union in context. He is careful to assert that material conditions, not the character or personality of the worker, were the cause of radicalism. Specifically, he argues that the development of monopoly capitalism in the latter part of the nineteenth century changed the nature of work and society. Rapid industrialization in the west, and technological innovations which displaced large segments of the working class, in turn created the conditions for fundamental conflict. Most important for Dubofsky, small-scale, local capital was replaced by large corporations. These new national corporations had no ties to the community and no knowledge of, or interest in, local customs, traditions, and conditions. Their size and dominant place in the economy made them almost invulnerable to small localized protest; their policies of centralized control meant that western managers had little power to intervene and act as buffers. Dubofsky suggests that "this divorce between ownership and local management, this geographical gulf between the worker and his ultimate employer, led to violent industrial conflict."[21]

But Dubofsky's use of western exceptionalism, or the belief that geography and location explain radicalism, leaves much to be explained. Radicalism in this period was not confined to the west, and such an explanation is especially difficult to apply to the IWW. Many of the delegates to the founding convention came from the eastern United States; half of the Canadian delegates came from Montreal. The first General Secretary-Treasurer of the union, William Trautman, was from Cincinnati.[22] And the IWW fought several of its most important battles in the east: Lawrence, Paterson, McKees Rocks, and Akron are only a few of the major eastern strikes that undermine western exceptionalism as an explanation for the IWW.

Dubofsky's framework of industrialization, corporatization, and technological change is also inadequate. Industrialization and technological change were hardly unique to the late nineteenth and early twentieth centuries. Indeed, the substitution of machine labour for human labour is an essential part of industrial capitalism, for making labour more productive through changes in the work process squeezes more profit out of the workers.[23] Why would this process suddenly push workers towards syndicalism in 1905? Pure and simple industrial unions would provide the stronger framework needed to fight the same battles against stronger employers. They might even be better equipped to protect their members than a radical organization, as Foner implies. The logical response to bad conditions or abuses is reform, not revolution; the desire for revolution surely suggests deep dissatisfaction with fundamental aspects of society. The IWW insisted on a radical transformation of society, and a very specific transformation at that. This is precisely the point Dubofsky does not adequately explain, Conlin seeks to ignore, and Foner, who is more sympathetic to the Communist movement, attempts to denigrate.

In his 1919 study of the IWW, Paul Brissenden made a similar appraisal of the contemporary liberal treatments of the union. His conclusions are compelling and applicable to the modern historiography:

> The writer is bound to say, however that he considers the liberal interpretation entirely inadequate. The liberal attitude is expressed and judgement pronounced when it has been said that the IWW is a social sore caused by, let us say, bad housing. It must be evident...that any organization which purposes a rearrangement of the status quo...is much more than that. The improvement of working conditions in the mines and lumber camps would tend to eliminate the cruder and less fundamental IWW activities, but it would not kill IWWism....We can only completely and fairly handle the IWW problem by dealing with its more fundamental tenets on their merits.[24]

These "fundamental tenets" include the organization of the unskilled, industrial unionism, and "the question of the sufficiency of political democracy." The most important, in Brissenden's view, was the demand that "some of our democracy...be extended from political into economic life. [The Wobblies] ask that industry be democratized by giving the workers—all grades of workers—exclusive control in its management."[25]

The primary question for the historian of the IWW then becomes, what prompted this specific drive for workers' control? It is fair, if not too helpful, to argue that capitalism in any form carries with it all that is necessary to create all types of resistance. And the IWW was the third mass movement in thirty years to challenge industrial capitalism in America, as it followed in the wake of Populism and the Knights of Labor. But the radicalism of the Industrial Workers of the World was different from that of the Populists and the Knights: it reflected the changes in the nature of capital and the lessons learned from the victories and defeats of those movements.

Most important was the change from competitive capitalism to monopoly capitalism. Having reached the limits of domestic growth by the end of the nineteenth century, corporations were forced to find new ways to increase and maintain profits. They did this in three ways. First, they sought to eliminate competition through mergers, price-fixing, and monopolies. Second, they used the government to regulate industry, restrict loans to new businesses, and limit competition. Third, they intensified the workday to make labour more productive. This was done in several ways. The open shop movement was launched to destroy unions and lower wages. Mechanization and factory work expanded, allowing management to replace skilled workers with semi- and unskilled ones. These were not new tactics, though their strength and intensity were greater than in earlier years. But when bosses tried to make work more productive, they were often stymied by the resistance of workers. Since these workers had a monopoly of skill and knowledge, they were often able to slow down and halt the drive to change the customary ways of doing the job. Management was then pushed to find new techniques for running factories and controlling the work process. These new methods, loosely gathered together under the headings of "scientific management," "de-skilling," and "efficiency," were designed to rob workers of their knowledge and their ability to control the job. The use of these managerial techniques was a new threat to workers, possible only with the advent of monopoly capitalism.[26]

The "father" of scientific management, Frederick Winslow Taylor, saw clearly that the chief impediment to intensifying labour and increasing profits was the monopoly of skill held by the work force. Skilled workers—carpenters, printers, machinists, coopers, steel puddlers, and masons, to name but a few—exerted a good deal of control over the job. Often they knew more about the production techniques than the boss did, for skills and traditions were passed on by other workers and the union, not the company. Craftsmen could often set the pace of work and the amount done in a day; they could, to a degree, decide what constituted a fair day's work, and could enforce minimum and maximum standards. Many shops would observe "Blue Monday," a day when workers recovering from weekend celebrations would not work to full capacity but would use the time to sharpen tools, plan the week's work schedule, and ease into the production routine. In the relative quiet of the cigar-making shop, workers would often appoint one of their comrades to read aloud to them as they worked. When the union controlled the apprentice program, it could limit the supply of skilled labour and help keep wages up. It would also ensure that new workers would be taught the principles of unionism along with the secrets of the trade. As highly trained craftsmen, workers were responsible for much more than the assembly-line production of "only the heads or points of nails," as Adam Smith suggested. They took an active part in the design of goods and in planning production: in many cases they, not the boss, would decide how something was to be made or produced. Management could not force more productivity from its employees if they controlled production—it could only "induce" workers to apply their "initiative" to yield the largest possible return. The solution to the problem of this informal workers' control over the work process was obvious to Taylor: managers would gather in all the traditional knowledge of the workers, and reduce this to a set of "rules, laws, and formulae." All of the planning formerly done by workers would now be done by management. Taylor recognized full well that his scheme "of a planning department to do the thinking for the men" hindered "independence, self-reliance, and originality in the individual." His answer highlights the entire thrust of capital in this era. Those who attacked Taylorism, he wrote, also "must take exception to the whole trend of modern industrial development."[27]

Other measures were combined with scientific management to break the power of skilled workers and intensify the exploitation of the unskilled. The open shop campaign flourished in this period. The drive system, which combined the principles of scientific management with a move to larger factories and the use of supervisors to make sure workers met high quotas, was created. Corporate welfare schemes were devised to take the edge off union organizing drives. These schemes included profit sharing plans, cafeterias, and workers' committees. Managers were professionalized and better trained to handle labour problems; together with sophisticated personnel departments, they strove to select suitable and acquiescent workers. The old hiring practices, often based on the informal networks of employees, simply left too much to chance. Company unions were established to circumvent real unions and foster an illusion of progressivism and class co-operation. Piecework, an old system condemned by Taylor as inefficient, was nonetheless joined with the new techniques to pressure workers to produce more. In their efforts to drive wages down, corporations went so far as to lobby the state for increased immigration, in order to swamp the market for unskilled labour. The newly created power of monopoly capitalism allowed business to embark on these fundamental changes to its relations with labour, changes Brissenden labelled the "Prussian method" of running industry. Contrary to Dubofsky's argument, this method was hardly confined to the west; its scope was marked off by the lines of class, not geography.[28]

Organized labour reacted to this threat in two ways. Many of the conservative leaders of the American Federation of Labor and the Canadian Trades and Labor Congress simply chose to retrench. Narrow battles to retain craft control were fought, as unions tried to protect their dwindling memberships from de-skilling and unemployment. Unskilled and immigrant workers were often viewed with alarm as competitors instead of potential allies, and a number of methods were used to keep them out of craft unions. Samuel Gompers himself symbolized and led a move away from any sort of radicalism or socialism. He moved the AFL towards a new respectability by co-operating with employers and refusing to fight for any demands save higher wages. This was an acceptance of the ground rules set by capitalism, for it meant workers could not challenge the employers' self-proclaimed right to ownership and control of the workplace. But another response developed as well. Rank and file AFL-TLC members, immigrants, women, the de-skilled, the unskilled—in short, those unable to find comfortable niches in craft union constituencies—often turned to radicalism and industrial unionism.

As the economic power of the new monopoly capitalists increased, so too did their political power. Increasingly, their voices were heard in the halls of government, their priorities and needs taken up by government officials. Despite public outrage at the trusts, the cartels, and the price-fixing that represented monopoly capitalism, successive governments in Canada and the United States did little to reduce the power of corporations. Though leaders such as Theodore Roosevelt and William Lyon Mackenzie King mouthed concern over the excesses of the trusts, they did virtually nothing to rein them in. It soon became clear that political action could not address the problem, for the governments responded to the lobbying of the powerful. In the United States, the Populist movement was utterly unable to force the state to defend farmers from the corporate giants. The Knights of Labor, despite their successes in focusing working class opposition and creating a strong working class culture, achieved little in the political arena. Despite their intense lobbying, neither the American Federation of Labor nor the Canadian Trades and Labor Congress had much influence on the governments of the day. Bill Haywood underscored the futility of labour's political efforts at the IWW's founding convention when he asked sarcastically, "If the American Federation of Labor spends $5,000 a year maintaining a legislative lobby and gets through absolutely none of the measures that they advocate, how long will it take the American Federation of Labor to bring the working class to the full product of its toil?" In contrast, he observed, the revolutionary industrial unionism of the Western Federation of Miners had "established in nearly all the cities through the west and the entire province of British Columbia the eight-hour day, and we did not have a legislative lobby to accomplish it."[29] Though Haywood seriously understated the state of affairs in B.C., where political lobbying had in fact resulted in an eight-hour law for miners, his comments reflected a growing perception that little could be gained by petitioning or electing a government. Workers throughout North America could point to any number of strikes and protests that had been settled by the bayonets and rifles of the government. And if Haywood had mis-stated the situation in B.C., it was still true that the Western Federation of Miners had turned to radicalism and direct action because its political efforts had largely failed.

Syndicalism was also an attempt to explain and combat a growing trend to conservatism and reformism in labour and socialist organizations. In North America, Britain, France, Germany, and Russia, radicals were alarmed by leaders who argued that capitalism could be reformed and that revolution was unnecessary. Socialists who could almost taste electoral victory were softening their belief in revolution to appeal to middle-class voters and were increasingly tempted to abandon the working class. If political action encouraged compromise and betrayal, syndicalists reasoned that the working class had to be prepared to go it alone and fight on its own terrain of the factory floor. Labour leaders were subject to similar pressures. As the heads of large organizations, they were powerful figures, often courted by capitalists and politicians. Negotiating contracts put them on nearly equal footing with the employer, and the very process of negotiating involved cutting deals and compromising. As successful bureaucrats, labour leaders had risen above the workers they represented and the need for revolution was no longer so obvious to them. Too often the men hailed as labour statesmen had lost their fire and were content to fit into the system and enjoy the fruits of capitalism. Even skilled workers who were not part of the union hierarchy had some stake in the present system, for their relative wealth was in part based on the labour of the unskilled and unorganized. Bill Haywood argued that

> As strange as it may seem to you, the skilled worker today is exploiting the laborer beneath him, the unskilled man, just as much as the capitalist is.... What I mean to demonstrate to you is that the skilled mechanic, by means of the pure and simple trades union, is exploiting the unskilled laborer.... The unskilled laborer has not been able to get into the skilled laborer's union because that union exacts that a man must needs have served a term of years as an apprentice. Again, there are unions in this country that exact an initiation fee, some of them as high as $500.... To demonstrate the point I wanted to get at, it is this: That the unskilled laborer's wages have been continually going down, and the prices of commodities have been continually going up, and that the skilled mechanic through his union has been able to hold his wages at a price...that has insured to him even at these high prices a reasonably decent living; but the laborer at the bottom, who is working for a dollar or a dollar and a quarter a day, has been ground into a state of destitution.[30]

Thus the skilled workers, through high initiation fees and apprenticeships, kept most workers out of the unions. This tended to make skilled labour scarcer, and enabled the unions to demand a higher price for their work. But it also doomed the mass of workers to increased exploitation; in effect, they subsidized the unionized workers with their lower wages.

It is, therefore, the confluence of several trends that explains the creation of the IWW in 1905. The AFL-TLC craft union structure was too weak to counter the new assaults of monopoly capitalism: only by uniting workers by industry could resistance be made effective. The base of the labour movement had to be expanded by organizing the unorganized and those thought unorganizable, not shrunk by excluding them and concentrating on a smaller number of craft veterans. Real changes, it appeared, could not be made through bargaining with the employers or lobbying the state; revolution was the only way to break their allied power. And since a mass movement was needed, radical groups had to seek a mass following among the working class or be doomed to impotence. If capital wanted to reduce the economic and political power of workers, it had to be opposed with complete political and economic democracy. Despite the specific grievances which triggered specific strikes, the explicit syndicalism of the IWW was caused by the advent of monopoly capital, the accompanying attack on labour, and the need felt for new forms of organization and new strategies.

It may be true that the model of "Prussianized industry" offered by Brissenden is inappropriate to the resource industries of western Canada and the United States, though research into the actual work process is largely lacking. The mines, logging camps, and railway construction sites that were IWW strongholds in B.C. could hardly be turned into modern factories complete with time-motion experts. And the theory of de-skilling, difficult to apply to miners and loggers, seems absurd when applied to railway section gangs, for pick and shovel work is virtually the definition of unskilled labour.

But the essence of the new system of production was not time-motion study, mechanization, or de-skilling. Its essence was in increasing the division of labour and in reducing the initiative of the workers over the work process to make labour more productive. All the old techniques—piece work, intimidation, bribery, and the like—were used in these industries. But in addition to these traditional methods, efforts to destroy workers' job control and assert managerial control were also used in lumber camps, mines, construction, and railway work. And, as Bryan Palmer points out, the new emphasis on efficiency and control spilled over into nearly every industrial field, giving managers an inspiration and an ideology to find new ways to reduce labour's share of wealth.[31]

Logan Hovis has demonstrated that in B.C. the monopoliza-
tion of mining and the depletion of resources forced companies to
mine lower-grade ores. This meant higher volumes of ore had to
be processed in order to sustain profits. It meant also that labour
costs had to be reduced and the productivity of miners raised; in
hardrock mining, from 1900 to 1930 productivity per worker increased by 500 per cent. The contract system and piece work were
adopted, but more importantly, "skill levels in hard-rock mining
were diluted . . . through the fragmentation of the work into tightly
defined and controlled components." In his unpublished paper,
Hovis cites the *Engineering and Mining Journal*, which observed in
1913 that "the itinerant, self-reliant miner, jack of all trades, and
master of several, was a disappearing breed"; instead,

> The new type of miner is not so intelligent, but he is more
> obedient and more industrious. He works generally for less
> than the scale established at such camps as Butte and
> Goldfield. By himself he is far less efficient, but as part of a
> system employing a multitude of bosses, he probably
> delivers a lower labor cost per ton. To many companies he
> is a more desirable employee than a skilled miner, even
> when the latter will work for the same wages.[32]

In his study of west coast logging, Richard Rajala has argued
that a similar process took place in the lumber industry. He
demonstrates that west coast logging came to be dominated by a
few large firms which adopted three approaches to increase "efficiency." First was the use of new power sources, especially elec-
tricity, and new systems of logging. Of these, the most important
was overhead yarding, which allowed machinery to replace
skilled chokermen and rigging slingers. As one Wobbly pointed
out, the use of these "flying machines" had a disastrous effect on
the workers, for they allowed production to double without
increasing the number of men employed, thus increasing profits
and unemployment simultaneously. The second approach was
the creation of logging engineering programs at universities. This
provided management with employees separate from the work
process and outside the union movement who would control and
oversee production. Finally, a variety of labour practices were
used to "enhance labour stability and convince loggers of the
reality of industrial partnership." These policies combined the
carrot of reform with the stick of repression. They included the

blacklist, piecework, improved conditions, insurance plans, and efforts to make logging communities more stable.[33]

In the building trades, long the bastion of the skilled craftsman, changes in production methods worked against the unions. Subcontracting and job specialization started early in the nineteenth century. Framing changed dramatically: the traditional craft of timber framing, which required great skill in joining large pieces of wood with mortise and tenon joints, was increasingly replaced by the now familiar balloon, or stud, framing. A miscalculation of an inch or so while timber framing could mean the ruin of a large and expensive piece of wood, but cutting too much off a two-by-four while balloon framing was of no real consequence. More and more, custom finishing work was done not by craftsmen on the site but in factories that turned out parts and trim by machine. Carpenters had only to tack the finished products to the wall. The IWW was quick to note the changes and their implications:

> The carpenter of twenty years ago...hewed, sawed, and carved out the pieces that go to make up a building's wooden work. The carpenter of today takes the product of a mill and puts it into place.... [Formerly] every man among them was capable of doing any part of the work to be done in the building.... The carpenter who comes to work on a modern building finds everything ready to his hand. There is no need for the elaborate tool chest of the days gone by and none for the old skilled hands and eye. Window cases, doors, partitions, molding, rails, and every conceivable thing to be used in the woodwork of the building are made and fitted at the mill. The carpenter fits them together. His work is not complicated.... He never was "bossed" before; now he is under the surveillance of an overseer. Before he needed more tools and more skill. So in the matter of work he is less a craftsman than a mechanic, less an independent factor than a cog in a wheel.... [T]he independence which his ability formerly gave him is lost to him forever.[34]

In the pages of *Solidarity*, Wobbly organizer Walker C. Smith noted that the increased use of concrete in houses, bridges, dams, streets, and office buildings meant that highly skilled craft workers would be replaced with labourers trained in the relatively unskilled tasks of making forms and pouring:

> From kiln workers to bricklayers, the workers are affected by

> concrete; the painter, carpenter, woodworker, plasterer, etc., all feel the jar, and the workers engaged in transportation also come in for their share of the industrial change.... [T]he displaced workers in turn become "unskilled" as their trade disappears.[35]

The evidence of efforts to control unskilled work is much less focused; indeed, we scarcely know how the railways were actually built. But despite the lack of research in this area, it is apparent that strenuous efforts were made to tightly control the work of muckers, navvies, and labourers. Taylor devoted a great deal of time to studying unskilled labour. His famous experiments with "Schmidt the Ox-man," for example, found ways to increase the loading of pig iron by hand from 12½ tons per worker per day to 47½ tons. Taylor was determined that "every single act of every workman can be reduced to a science.... there was such a thing as the science of shovelling." He demonstrated that shovelling could be improved by supplying shovels of different designs and sizes to ensure each worker hoisted the ideal weight of 27 pounds per shovel-full. Foremen would insist that the proper shovel be used and would ensure that workers use the "exact methods which should be employed to use their strength to the very best advantage." Covington Hall, a Wobbly writer, pointed out that while "Schmidt's" work load increased by nearly 400 per cent, his daily wage was raised by only about 60 per cent; if his wages were figured on a price per ton, they actually fell 60 per cent under Taylorism. Hall also noted that "the next set of Ox Men to be 'scientifically educated' will be the highly skilled and superior Ox Men on the railroads."[36]

Frank Gilbreth, the founder of motion study made famous by the book and the Clifton Webb movie *Cheaper by the Dozen*, applied his principles to unskilled labour. Two hundred and thirty-one rules were devised for the relatively uncomplicated task of mixing concrete. Rule 198 suggests how far the quest for managerial control would go: "When men shovel against a plank always use a square pointed shovel. Use a round pointed shovel at all other times." The ideas of Gilbreth and Taylor travelled far from home: in 1912, a writer in the Spokane paper of the IWW observed,

> The "shovel stiffs" in New Westminster, B.C., are being treated to a dose of Taylor's "scientific management." They

have to swing their shovels in a certain way, with a specified amount of sand therein, and fill the wagons within a set time. If Christian Science can now be invoked to cause the slaves to keep their minds from such things as food, clothes, and shelter, the plutes will have succeeded in securing perfect profit producers.[37]

On the railway, where, as *Industrial Canada* rhapsodized, "the air resounds with the grinding of steamshovels, the blasting of rock, and all the uproar attending such a colossal task," the system of sub-contracting and station men constituted a virtual piecework system in the construction of the grade and the laying of track. Edmund Bradwin, in his early study of railway construction, concluded that "the whole contract system is top-heavy and lop-sided—it gives good pickings to the sub-contractors, but it begrudges conditions and a human wage to the navvy who handles the barrow and shovel." In this respect, the piece-work and quota system of the railways resembled that of the factory.[38]

Railway engineers also began to figure ways to make construction more efficient. W.M. Camp, a member of the American Society of Civil Engineers, and an editor of the *Railway and Engineering Review*, echoed Taylor and Gilbreth in his 1904 handbook, *Notes on Track*:

> In these days when so much of industry is dependent upon the activities of corporations, and when labor is becoming more and more divided, men in general will take less and less interest in that which they engage to do, except in what may appear to promise them more or less direct returns in higher compensation or in reputation. Obviously, then, there will be a larger demand for men whose occupation it shall be to maintain a close watch on details, with a view to turn aside all the undirected and misdirected tendencies which might lead to extravagance, inefficiency, or whatever in the end might operate depressingly upon dividends, which constitute the ultimate aim of the projectors of railroads.[39]

In words reminiscent of Taylor's admonition that the workers "possess [the] mass of traditional knowledge, a large part of which is not in the possession of the management," Camp writes,

> I consider that there are many roadmasters and section foremen who have more to do with track engineering than some men commonly known as civil engineers.... The

experience necessary to teach such knowledge must be had by actual contact with the work.... There are men who have never so much as sweat a drop in any kind of service...eager to propose what they think to be some track improvement; and as a rule their ideas on improvements amount to about as much as their services have.

But the well-trained supervisor, one in whom the theoretical knowledge of the engineer and practical experience of the worker were combined, would "find opportunity to reduce the expenses of his department without curtailing its effectiveness. By such supervision it is often possible to increase the output of labor in such a way that the laborer is unconscious of it."[40]

Just as Taylor and Gilbreth held that the supervisor and not the worker should make the decisions concerning which tool to use for which job, so does Camp outline for engineers ways to organize tools and their use. He suggests, for example, that just as many tools as necessary should be placed at each section, "for an over-abundance of tools has a tendency to make foremen careless of them." This small note implies a great deal. The engineer, responsible for a number of sections, will determine the type and number of tools each is to use in the course of a day's work; he will know how to organize the work better than the men on the section. It also points out the special role of the engineer: even more than the foreman, he is assumed to have allied himself with the company and is pledged to look after its best interests.

The engineer is also charged with ensuring that each tool operates at peak efficiency. This seems an odd requirement with tools such as picks and shovels, but Camp observes that a "shovel blade worn off to less than 9 ins. length becomes...unprofitable. Every day's work with such a shovel will...lose to the company at least one third of the price of a new shovel." Double-bitted axes are preferable to single-bitted, for the latter "comes in so handy for a wedge that the head is usually found badly battered from hammer blows." The shovel is to be of specific dimensions, in order to provide the most efficient use:

> The proper size of the blade is about 12 ins. long and 9½ or 10 ins. wide at the working edge or "point." The handle should be about 27 ins. long (direct measurement), from the top of the blade, and so crooked that when the blade is in position for filling, on a level surface, the end of the handle

is 18 ins. above the ground. This is the height of the knee of
a man of ordinary size when the leg is bent as in the act of
shoving the blade forward to fill it.... The weight should not
exceed 6½ lbs.... The thickness of the blade for light work is
1/16 in. but for railroad service it should be at least 3/32 in.

Foremen, Camp suggests, should teach the men under them to
shovel properly, for "one would naturally suppose that any man
could learn to shovel dirt without instructions; but such is not the
case." The foreman must also make sure that the proper-shaped
pick is used for specific tasks, and that an eight-pound hammer is
used for general section work, while one of nine or ten pounds is
used for laying track. While Camp recognizes that all men are not
equal in their ability to work, he nonetheless gives estimates of the
amount of work that crews should be capable of. A man should be
able to load twenty cubic yards of gravel onto a flat car in ten
hours; a standard crew of fifty-six men should be able to lay a mile
of track in the same period.[41]

Foremen had the responsibility of assigning workers to specific
tasks in order to make them "specialists" and thereby reduce
labour costs through an increased division of labour. Camp
observes that though section labour was considered "the most
ordinary type of labor", in fact, "an expert trackman is a skilled
laborer, a tradesman—fully as much so as is a carpenter, a smith,
or a mason. Men cannot become expert at all kinds of track labor
in a few months. A good, bright man would do well if he gained
the necessary experience in two years." But the railroad companies preferred to use cheap immigrant labour and "the low rate
of wages paid has bid for nothing better than common labor"; in
these circumstances, it was necessary to define closely the job of
each worker and train foremen and engineers to teach and watch
them.[42]

The railways were also quick to devise new ways to discipline
workers. The use of "brownie points" was started by the railways
and is continued today. In common usage, "brownie points" are
allegedly awarded to fawning or overzealous employees who are
eager to win favour with their superiors. On the railways, however, they are demerit points given for infractions of the rules and
procedures. The points go on an employee's personnel record,
and if enough are collected, the employee may be fired. The system was first used by George R. Brown of the Fall Brook Railroad

as a way of disciplining workers without the inconvenience of suspending them, and became known as the Brown system. The strength of the system, according to Brown, was that "the good men are retained, developed, benefited, and encouraged, and the culls are got rid of to the betterment of the service all around." Another railway manager noted that the system tended to make the employees "feel that you are their friend rather than their natural enemy; that your interests are mutual and that their acts reflect credit or discredit upon you." The system was created in the 1890s, and was in place on the CPR by 1908. Its paternalism was another way to try to reduce conflict on the job and create a loyal cadre of workers who would be eager to follow the rules and regulations laid down by the managers.[43]

Not every employer adopted the new techniques. Taylor himself often complained that not a single factory had actually adopted his system wholeheartedly. Frank Leonard, in his recent analysis of the Grand Trunk Pacific Railway, has concluded that the failure of the company to adopt "modern" management procedures led to its financial ruin.[44]

But the IWW was keenly aware that this was the new direction of capitalism, and that it would soon affect all workers, directly or indirectly. At the founding convention, Wobblies argued that capital was out to break the control of workers. The manifesto issued to call the convention held that

> The *great facts* of present industry are the displacement of human skill by machines and the increase of capitalist power through concentration in the possession of the tools with which wealth is produced and distributed....New machines, ever replacing less productive ones, wipe out whole trades and plunge new bodies of workers into the ever-growing army of tradeless, hopeless unemployed.[45]

Haywood thundered to the audience,

> Don't you know that there is not an employing capitalist or corporation manufactory in this country that if it were possible would not operate his or its entire plant or factory by machines and dispose of every human being employed?... Remember that to-day there are no skilled mechanics.... There is a train of specialized men that do just their part, that is all. The machine is the apprentice of yesterday; the machine is the journeyman of to-day.[46]

Even those whose trade was not directly affected were threatened by the new industrial system. The IWW warned that workers who despised the displaced tramp were facing their own future. The unemployed hobo was "a worker before he was a tramp. A machine took his job and he left for another city to seek employment. The machine got there first. . . . The march of the machine is steady. It is even now upon you. Tomorrow you may be a tramp."[47]

The founders of the IWW viewed their North American form of syndicalism as the logical response to the new assaults of capital. It is in a sense irrelevant to ask if a single railway navvy along the Fraser River joined the IWW in response to the de-skilling of his job. Probably only a small number of those who supported and joined the union did so because of a commitment to syndicalism and a carefully reasoned critique of monopoly capitalism. Workers joined the IWW because it was there. But the union was there because its founders were aware of the dangerous, autocratic power of capital and the state. The IWW was formed to combat the "Prussian" method of organizing production, even if workers often joined it for the same reason they continue to join unions: to fight immediate battles to improve conditions.

Notes for Chapter 1

1. Melvyn Dubofsky, *We Shall Be All: A History of the Industrial Workers of the World*. New York: Quadrangle/The New York Times Book Company, 1969, pp. 74-76; Paul Brissenden, *The IWW: A Study of American Syndicalism*. 1919. Reprint. New York: Russell and Russell Inc. 1957, pp. 59-67.

2. *The Founding Convention of the Industrial Workers of the World, Proceedings*. 1905. Reprint. New York: Merit Publishers, 1969, pp. 1-6.

3. William D. Haywood, *Bill Haywood's Book: The Autobiography of William D. Haywood*. 1929. Reprint. New York: International Publishers, 1977, p. 181; *Founding Convention*, p. 1; Ray Ginger, *The Bending Cross: A Biography of Eugene V. Debs*. New Brunswick: Rutgers University Press, 1949, p. 238.

4. Larry Peterson, "The One Big Union in International Perspective: Revolutionary Industrial Unionism, 1900-1925," *Labour/Le Travailleur* 7 (Spring 1981) pp. 41-66, gives a helpful definition of syndicalism. Briefly, its tenets are an emphasis on decentralization; opposition to political parties and parliamentary politics; advocacy of the general strike as the means to the revolution; a vision of a new society as a federation of

economic organizations based on the structure of craft and industry. See Dubofsky, pp. 166-170, for a similar appraisal. See also Philip Foner, *The History of the Labor Movement in the United States*, Volume 4, *The Industrial Workers of the World, 1905-1917*. New York, International Publishers, 1965, pp. 20-23.

5. The quote on industries taking the place of the state is cited in Dubofsky, p. 167. The attack on state socialism is in the *Industrial Worker* (hereafter *IW*), 19 June 1913; Brissenden, pp. 368-369.

6. Haywood cited in Joyce L. Kornbluh, ed., *Rebel Voices: An IWW Anthology*. 1964. Reprint. Ann Arbor: University of Michigan Press, 1972, p. 36. It is important to understand just what the IWW meant by direct action. Many critics have claimed that in rejecting political action, the IWW believed that the state was irrelevant. This is not true, as the preceding quotes indicate. The IWW was not apolitical, for wanting to smash the state is a very political program. It is not a *parliamentary* political program, and this is the important distinction. It is true that Wobblies held electoral politics in disdain, but they were all too aware of the necessity of destroying the state if workers were to be free. By direct action, the union meant action that workers did themselves without the mediation of the state, politicians, or political parties. This meant directing the efforts of workers to the workplace. Direct action could take many forms: strikes, slow-downs, sabotage, indeed anything that workers could apply themselves—directly—to attack the system.

7. Haywood cited in Kornbluh, pp. 44-51.

8. Andre Tridon, *The New Unionism*, cited in Kornbluh, p. 36.

9. Joseph R. Conlin, *Bread and Roses Too: Studies of the Wobblies*. Westport: Greenwood Press, 1969, p. 82. For a critique of Conlin, see William Preston, "Shall This Be All? U.S. Historians Versus William D. Haywood, *et al.*," *Labor History*, Volume 12 Number 3 (Spring 1971). Peterson, following Conlin, holds that the IWW was not syndicalist; like Conlin, he is wrong. He is quite correct, however, to insist that the Canadian One Big Union was not a syndicalist organization. Readers should not confuse the Canadian OBU with the IWW's reference to itself as the "One Big Union." The Canadian OBU was formed in 1919, and its leaders explicitly rejected the ideology of the IWW.

10. *Founding Convention*, p. 7. In attempting to make the IWW into a pure and simple industrial union, Conlin misinterprets a number of ideas. He insists that the French model of syndicalism, based on craft unions and committed to a policy of "boring from within" the conservative unions, is the definitive one. Insofar as the IWW deviated from the French model, Conlin holds that it was not syndicalist. As proof, he cites William Foster's Syndicalist League, which did try to infiltrate the AFL and work within it. Unfortunately for Conlin, Foster himself argued that both the IWW and the League were syndicalist, and he held that the difference was only one of tactics.

11. Conlin, p. 90. This argument may also obscure some very real differences between AFL leaders and the rank and file. David Montgomery has argued, if a little too optimistically, that the IWW in fact represented part of a swing towards radicalism among many workers in this period. See David Montgomery, *Workers' Control in*

America: Studies in the History of Work, Technology, and Labor Struggles. 1979. Reprint. Cambridge: Cambridge University Press, 1984, and *The Fall of the House of Labor: The Workplace, the State, and American Labor Activism, 1865-1925.* Cambridge: Cambridge University Press, 1987.

12. *IW*, 22 May 1913.

13. Foner, *The IWW*, pp. 470-472.

14. See Dubofsky, pp. 164-165; Foner, *The IWW*, pp. 378, 470-472; John G. Brooks, *American Syndicalism: The IWW.* 1913. Reprint. New York: Arno and The New York Times, 1969, pp. 87-88, 130; Barbara Garson, *All the Livelong Day: The Meaning and Demeaning of Routine Work.* New York: Doubleday, 1975. Reprint. Middlesex: Penguin Books, 1977, pp. 74-75; *Founding Convention*, pp. 111-112, 577, 589; Brissenden, pp. 85-86.

15. Cited in Frederick W. Thompson and Patrick Murfin, *The IWW: Its First Seventy Years, 1905-1975.* Chicago: The Industrial Workers of the World, 1976, p. 154.

16. *Founding Convention*, pp. 125, 278-279, 576; Foner, *The IWW*, p. 121; Dubofsky, pp. 7-8, 71-73, 86-87. Foner, *The IWW*, p. 471; Dubofsky, p. 150. For a contemporary attack on the policy of attracting workers to unions by offering them a "deal," see Eric Mann, "Unions Absent on Sunday Are Dead on Monday," *New York Times*, 1 September 1986, p. 15. Note especially the new twist of offering low-interest credit cards. *Founding Convention*, pp. 117-118.

17. Joseph Ettor, *Proceedings of the Tenth Convention of the IWW*, cited in Foner, *The IWW*, pp. 471-472.

18. *Founding Convention*, pp. 117-118.

19. Philip Foner, *History of the Labor Movement in the United States*, Volume 2, *From the Founding of the AF of L to the Emergence of American Imperialism.* New York: International Publishers, 1964, pp. 389-390, 398-401; Foner, Volume 3, *The Policies and Practices of the AF of L, 1900-1909.* New York: International Publishers, 1964, p. 27; Paul Buhle, *Marxism in the USA from 1870 to the Present Day.* London: Verso, 1987, pp. 49-57. DeLeon is quoted from the *Founding Convention*, p. 151.

20. Emma Goldman, *Living My Life.* Reprint. 1931. New York: Dover Publications, 1970, Volume 1, p. 52.

21. Dubofsky, pp. 19-36; the quote is from p. 23.

22. *Founding Convention*, pp. 22-24, 538, 595-597.

23. See Karl Marx, *Capital.* Moscow: Progress Publishers, 1954. In Volume 1, part IV, chapter 12, Marx argues that "The technical and social conditions of the process and consequently the very mode of production must be revolutionised, before the productiveness of labour can be increased." See also Marx, *Wage Labour and Capital.* This argument and the appreciation of Brissenden which follows are outlined in Preston, "Shall This Be All?"

24. Brissenden, pp. 18-19.

25. Brissenden, pp. 19-20.

26. An extensive literature examines the rise and impact of monopoly capitalism. Some books that are especially useful are James Livingstone, *Origins of the Federal Reserve System: Money, Class, and Corporate Capitalism, 1890-1913.* Ithaca: Cornell University Press, 1983; Allen Trachtenberg,

The Incorporation of America: Culture and Society in the Guilded Age. New York: Hill and Wang, 1982; James Weinstein, *The Corporate Ideal in the Liberal State, 1900-1918.* Boston: Beacon Press, 1968; David Noble, *America by Design: Science, Technology, and the Rise of Corporate Capitalism.* New York: Knopf, 1977. For Canada, the following are useful: Tom Traves, *The State and Enterprise.* Toronto: University of Toronto Press, 1979; Alvin Finkel, *Business and Social Reform in the Thirties.* Toronto: Lorimer, 1979; Paul Craven, *"An Impartial Umpire": Industrial Relations and the Canadian State, 1900-1911.* Toronto: University of Toronto Press, 1980.

27. See Montgomery, *Workers' Control* and *Fall of the House of Labor;* Braverman; G.S. Kealey, *Toronto Workers Respond to Industrial Capitalism, 1867-1892.* Toronto: University of Toronto Press, 1980. See pp. 53-54 for "Blue Monday". Many of the essays in Craig Heron and Robert Storey, eds., *On the Job: Confronting the Labour Process in Canada.* Kingston and Montreal: McGill-Queen's University Press, 1986, discuss workers' control. Frederick W. Taylor, "The Principles of Scientific Management," in *Scientific Management.* 1911. Reprint. Westport: Greenwood Press, 1972, pp. 32-33. For a more detailed analysis of this process and its implications, see Braverman, especially pp. 3-139; Taylor, "Principles," pp. 36-37; Taylor, "Shop Management," in *Scientific Management,* p. 146.

28. For the drive system, see David Gordon, Richard Edwards and Michael Reich, *Segmented Work, Divided Workers: The Historical Transformation of Labor in the United States.* Cambridge: Cambridge University Press, 1982, pp. 128-135. Brissenden, p. 20. See Preston for a similar observation. For descriptions of the measures taken to intensify work and break unions, see Foner, *The AFL, 1900-1909,* especially chapters 2 and 7; Montgomery, *Workers' Control in America,* pp. 32-47, 91-112; Montgomery, *Fall of the House of Labor;* Braverman, especially part 1. See Robert Wiebe, *The Search for Order, 1877-1920.* New York: Hill and Wang, 1967, pp. 133-163, for the "revolution in values" that urbanization and industrialization spawned and that helped to establish a social context for the changes in industry. For similar analyses in the Canadian context, see Bryan D. Palmer, *Working-Class Experience: The Rise and Reconstitution of Canadian Labour, 1800-1980.* Toronto: Butterworth and Company, 1983, pp. 141-157; G.S. Kealey, "The Structures of Canadian Working-Class History," *Lectures in Canadian Working-Class History.* Toronto: Committee on Canadian Labour History and New Hogtown Press, 1985, pp. 28-31, edited by W.J.C. Cherwinski and G.S. Kealey; Craig Heron, "The Crisis of the Craftsman: Hamilton's Metal Workers in the Early Twentieth Century." *Labour/Le Travailleur* 6 (Autumn 1980); Bryan D. Palmer, *A Culture in Conflict: Skilled Workers and Industrial Capitalism in Hamilton, Ontario, 1860-1914.* Montreal: McGill-Queen's University Press, 1979, especially chapter 7. For Canadian immigration policy, see Donald Avery, *"Dangerous Foreigners": European Immigrant Workers and Labour Radicalism in Canada, 1896-1932.* Toronto: McClelland and Stewart, 1980. For more on skilled and unskilled labour, see Ian McKay, "Class Struggle and Merchant Capital: Craftsmen and Labourers on the Halifax Waterfront 1850-1902," and Craig Heron, "Hamilton Steelworkers and the Rise of Mass Production," both in *The*

Character of Class Struggle: Essays in Canadian Working-Class History, 1850-1985. Bryan D. Palmer, ed. Toronto: McClelland and Stewart, 1986. See also Palmer's introduction. For the development of Canadian monopoly capitalism, see R.T. Naylor, *The History of Canadian Business, 1867-1914.* Two volumes. Toronto: James Lorimer, 1975. See especially Volume 2, chapter 14.

29. *Founding Convention*, p. 154.

30. *Founding Convention*, pp. 575-576.

31. Palmer, *Working-Class Experience*, p. 140.

32. Logan W. Hovis, "The Origins of 'Modern Mining' in the Western Cordillera, 1880-1930." Paper presented at B.C. Studies Convention, Victoria, November, 1986, pp. 20-21; *B.C. Mines Report*, 1947, gives the figures for increased productivity.

33. Richard Rajala, "The Rude Science: Technology and Management in the West Coast Logging Industry, 1890-1930." Paper presented at B.C. Studies Convention, Victoria, November 1986, pp. 3, 17-18. *IW*, 11 June 1910. H. A. Logan, in *Trade Unions in Canada: Their Development and Functioning.* Toronto: Macmillan, 1948, pp. 280-281, argues that by the early twentieth century, logging was monopolized and subject to mechanization and speed-ups.

34. Sean Wilentz, *Chants Democratic: New York City and the Rise of the American Working Class, 1788-1850.* New York: Oxford University Press, 1984; Ian McKay, *The Craft Transformed: An Essay on the Carpenters of Halifax, 1885-1985.* Halifax: Holdfast Press, 1985; Philip Langdon, "Not Log Cabins," *Atlantic*, December 1988, pp. 80-82; *Industrial Union Bulletin*, 9 March 1907.

35. *Solidarity*, 19 February 1910.

36. Taylor, "Principles," pp. 64-66, 68-69; *Solidarity*, 18 March 1911. The "best advantage," of course, was defined as "most profitable to the boss," and purposely denied workers the ability to decide what their own "best advantage" might be. As Joe Cherwinski has wryly observed, workers paid by the hour might well prefer to load gravel with a pitch fork, not a shovel. The quip points out the huge gulf between the desires of the boss and the workers.

37. Gilbreth cited in Harold R. Pollard, *Developments in Managerial Thought.* London: William Heineman, 1974, p. 20; *IW*, 29 August, 1912.

38. *Industrial Canada*, October 1911, pp. 361-362. Edmund Bradwin, *The Bunkhouse Man: A Study of Work and Pay in the Camps of Canada, 1903-1914.* 1928. Reprint. Toronto: University of Toronto Press, 1972, p. 201.

39. W.M. Camp, *Notes on Track, Construction and Maintenance.* 1903. Second revised edition, Chicago: Published by author, 1904, pp. 1-2.

40. Camp, pp. 3, 637.

41. Camp, pp. 638, 641, 689, 639, 732, 188.

42. Camp, p. 1080.

43. Camp, pp. 1098-1101. No doubt the common usage of "brownie points" is connected to the image of "brown-nosing" and the belief that the girls who join the youth organization known as Brownies (from the name for a good-natured goblin) are eager to please. Webster's *Third New International Dictionary* defines "brownie points" as a demerit given railway employees, but its *Ninth New Collegiate Dictionary* defines them as

"a credit regarded as earned esp. by currying favour with a superior," and dates this usage from 1967.

44. Frank Leonard, Ph.D. thesis, "'A Thousand Blunders': The Grand Trunk Pacific Railway Company and Northern British Columbia, 1902-1919." York University, 1988.

45. *Founding Convention*, pp. 3-4.

46. *Founding Convention*, p. 579.

47. *IW*, 22 May 1913.

CHAPTER 2

Rallying 'Round the Standard in British Columbia

Canadian historians have been less inclined to examine the Industrial Workers of the World than their American counterparts. Those who have studied it have avoided using the framework of monopoly capitalism to guide their analysis, and they tend to play down the significance of the sharply focused critique put forward by the union. This is largely because Canadian labour history has been written by two "generations" of historians. The second generation, typified by the work of Gregory S. Kealey and Bryan D. Palmer, has taken its lead from the work of British Marxist historians—notably E.P. Thompson and Eric Hobsbawm—and Americans such as Herbert Gutman and David Montgomery. They have been quick to adapt these ideas to Canadian history, but their work has tended to focus on the skilled artisans of eastern Canada in the early years of industrialization. While they have on occasion extended their theories to the age of monopoly capitalism that followed, their research and interest have tended to remain rooted in the Ontario of the nineteenth century.

The history of the early twentieth century and the west has largely become the province of the so-called first generation. This set of historians has tended to play down class conflict and uses instead the theoretical framework of liberalism and social democracy. Among other things, this framework views radicalism as an aberration; it owes a great deal to the structural-functionalism of Talcott Parsons and N.J. Smelser. As E.P. Thompson has pointed out, this school regards unrest and class consciousness as "a bad thing...since everything which disturbs the harmonious coexistence of groups performing different 'social roles' (and which thereby retards economic growth) is to be deplored as an 'unjustified disturbance symptom.'" Rejecting radicalism as an appropriate response, these historians tend to use the "social sore" theory dismissed by Brissenden. Thus David Bercuson, in his study of the Canadian One Big Union, ironically cites William Pritchard to assure readers that "only fools make revolutions, wise men conform to them." He then argues that radicalism was a western phenomenon caused by specific correctable abuses, notably coal mines that "were among the most dangerous in the world." In an effort to make radicalism into an individual reaction instead of a logical, rational response to an alienating system, Bercuson suggests that revolt grew, in part, because thwarted ambitions and frustrated family lives created a climate in which outside agitators could flourish.[1]

This explanation suffers from the same flaws as the liberal versions attacked by Brissenden. It is unable to explain the particular syndicalism of the IWW and it does not explain eastern radicalism, or the antecedents and descendents of the IWW. Preferring to see radicalism as an extreme protest against conditions that could easily be rectified by a liberal or social democratic state, Bercuson explicitly denies any role to monopoly capitalism. He asserts that the western Canadian coal industry, for example, was composed of a mass of small producers employing a few men, and argues that these small mines could not make use of the new managerial techniques. But as Allen Seager has pointed out, "the coal industry in B.C. was completely dominated by two or three large firms who held extraordinary concessions."[2] If western mines were indeed among the most dangerous in the world surely they were so, in large part, because of the concern for sustained production and the ability of monopoly capital to fight unions effectively. Furthermore, the links between the state and capital in British Columbia have been drawn by writers as diverse as Margaret Ormsby and Martin Robin. The close ties between the two suggest that the state was unable or unwilling to enact reforms precisely because of the dominance of monopoly capital.[3]

The second generation has stressed working class culture and unity, but in doing so it often fails to differentiate between the different responses of the left and labour movements within the region. Robert McDonald makes a similar mistake, albeit for opposite reasons, in his analysis of Vancouver workers. Posing an over-simplified dichotomy between city and country, he suggests that "urbanism" somehow created a less radical, monolithic working class that was markedly different from the working class of the hinterland. But this position is only tenable if the differences and splits in the Vancouver labour movement are ignored.[4]

Ross McCormack, in the most detailed account of western

Canadian radicalism to date, has presented a model of three responses to capital: reform, rebellion, and revolution. While his argument that each was a reaction to the boom conditions of the western frontier relies too heavily on the assumption of western exceptionalism, it is not necessarily in opposition to the theory of monopoly capitalism described above.

His careful attempt to isolate separate strands of the workers' movement is not without difficulties. McCormack is well aware of the problems, pointing out that

> Reformers and revolutionaries employed the same tactics. Revolutionaries and rebels subscribed to one ideology. And from time to time men and women blurred distinctions even further by enlisting with two or more of these tendencies at the same time, however contradictory such behaviour might appear.[5]

Despite this warning, the picture of conflicting and competing responses is more accurate than Bercuson's portrait of regional unity, or McDonald's Vancouver/hinterland dichotomy. The British Columbia labour movement was in flux in the pre-war years, turning sometimes to labourism, sometimes to syndicalism, sometimes to socialism, as it attempted to find solutions to the new problems presented by monopoly capitalism. Labour had a variety of options open to it, and had not yet decided on or been structured into either a moderate and reformist course or a revolutionary one.

But Canadian historians have been loath to look seriously at the IWW. The union is ignored in the survey texts of Kenneth McNaught and J.L. Finlay and D.N. Sprague, while Ralph Allen's popular history, *Ordeal by Fire*, incorrectly states that the IWW became the One Big Union in 1918, with the Social Democratic Party of Canada as its "political arm." *Twentieth Century Canada*, the collective work of J.L. Granatstein, Craig Brown, Blair Neatby, and the labour historians Irving Abella and David Bercuson, makes only passing references to the IWW in the text, and refers to it as the International Workers of the World in the index. Desmond Morton, in the labour history survey *Working People*, concludes that the "Wobblies survived chiefly to give organized labour a healthy jab of respectability." He goes so far as to cite the aggressively pro-business *Canadian Annual Review* to suggest that the IWW's platform was merely a "pestilent body of undefined anarchist principles from the United States." In his account of B.C. unionism, Paul Phillips claims the union was "spawned" by "wretched conditions," and "left almost no permanent mark on the B.C. labour movement," despite his own observation that it was at one time the largest union in the province, and despite its obvious links to the OBU, the Communist Party, and the left-led CIO unions in the province. The only monograph on the IWW in Canada is Jack Scott's colourful celebration *Plunderbund and Proletariat*, which serves as a popular introduction to the history of the union's famous free speech fights and major strikes in B.C.. To date, the most complete scholarly work on the IWW is the twenty pages given to it in McCormack's *Reformers, Rebels, and Revolutionaries*.[6]

But the union played an important part in the B.C. labour movement. Within six months of its founding convention, the IWW had a local of miners at Phoenix; by the end of 1906, other locals were established in Greenwood, Victoria, Moyie, and Vancouver. By 1907, there were five locals in the Kootenay region, and at least three in Vancouver.[7] Following Big Bill Haywood's enjoinder that the IWW was "going down in the gutter to get at the mass of workers and bring them up to a decent plane of living," Wobblies organized miners, loggers, farm workers, longshoremen, and road and railway construction workers. Unlike many AFL unions in B.C., the IWW organized among all ethnic groups, including Asians. As one member put it, "all this anti-Japanese talk comes from the employing class. Which is better: to have the Japanese in the Union with you, or to force him to scab on the outside?" The word "Wobbly," a nickname for IWW members, humourously illustrates the union's efforts to combat racism. A Chinese restaurant keeper in Vancouver in 1911 supported the union and would extend credit to members. Unable to pronounce the letter "w," he would ask if a man was in the "I Wobble Wobble." Local members jokingly referred to themselves as part of the "I Wobbly Wobbly," and by the time of the Wheatland strike of 1913, "Wobbly" had become a permanent moniker for workers who carried the red card. Mortimer Downing, a Wobbly who first explained the etymology, noted that the nickname "hints of a fine, practical internationalism, a human brotherhood based on a community of interests and of understanding."[8]

The IWW actively organized women and did not exclude them from important positions in the union. Women such as Lucy Parsons and Elizabeth Gurley Flynn went on speaking tours of B.C.; Alice Harling and M. Gleason headed local 44 in Victoria. Edith Frenette, a friend of Gurley Flynn, was an active organizer throughout the Pacific Northwest who took part in the first important IWW free speech fight, that of Missoula, Montana, in 1909. Some years later, she was a participant in the tragic events in Everett, Washington, where a number of Wobblies were murdered by vigilantes and deputies as they tried to leave a ferry and join a free speech fight. In June 1911, Frenette gave birth to a daughter, Stella Bonnie, in a desolate lumber camp in Holberg, B.C., near the northern tip of Vancouver Island. The baby was given a red diaper baptism: at its regular business meeting, Local Union 380 of the IWW issued Stella union card number 11014. In November, Edith was working with her husband and brother-in-law to organize the loggers of Port Alberni. When company thugs and AFL supporters threatened to pull the brother-in-law off the soapbox he used to address a crowd of workers, she

> butted in and got on the box myself. This was something they hadn't figured on as they were hardly prepared to beat up a woman. When I got my breath I sailed into them and they quieted like any other whipped cur, only a few snarls being heard from them. I called them a few choice names and appealed to their manhood if they had any.

After she quelled the mob, the camp resolutions and grievances were read out and adopted unanimously by the assembled workers. Frenette's courage and skill could not protect her, however, from personal tragedy. In March 1912, Stella Bonnie died as the result of a fall. The *Industrial Worker* was quick to "join all other rebels in extending sympathy to our bereaved fellow workers in the hour of their affliction."[9]

The union was active in the hinterlands of the province. John Riordan, a Canadian delegate to the founding convention, had insisted the union be named the Industrial Workers of the World instead of the proposed Industrial Workers of America. He continued to organize in the Boundary area and served on the General Executive Board of the IWW during its first year. Riordan, along with the secretary-treasurer, William Trautman, was instrumental in opposing the corrupt and conservative administration of the union's first and only president, C.O. Sherman. Sherman and his cronies were draining the union treasury by submitting inflated vouchers for travel expenses. With Trautman organizing for the union, Riordan was left alone to try to stem the flow of money. Outvoted and outmanoeuvred by Sherman and his supporters, "Honest John" fought back by stamping "for graft" on all the travel vouchers. Later, he joined with others to throw out Sherman, and ensure that the IWW would remain a revolutionary organization. This stance, however, put B.C. Wobblies in opposition to the leadership of the Western Federation of Miners, and the two unions competed for the allegiance of miners in the province. The Phoenix local first sided with the Sherman faction, but later applied to be reinstated in the IWW. Other locals stayed with the Federation, but supported the IWW position. Greenwood, for example, sent Fred Heslewood to the 1906 IWW convention, where he joined with Riordan and others to challenge WFM conservatives. In 1907, the local supported the Goldfield, Nevada Wobblies, Joe Smith and Morrie Preston, who were being framed for the murder of a restaurant owner during a gold miners' strike.[10]

The IWW exerted an influence in the Boundary area that far exceeded the number of miners on the union's rolls. Militants in the WFM as well as the United Mine Workers of America were often sympathetic to the IWW and syndicalism, and working class solidarity usually cut across lines of trade union jurisdiction in the mining communities. In September 1907, miners from Grand Forks, Greenwood, Phoenix, Motherlode, Summit, and Boundary Falls met for a joint picnic at Curlew Lake. The festivities included the stoning of effigies of the Pinkerton spies James McParland and Harry Orchard, who had conspired with the state government to frame WFM leaders Moyer, Haywood, and Pettibone on a murder charge in Idaho. In 1909, the Wobbly organizer Elizabeth Gurley Flynn made a speaking tour of the district, while the Grand Forks local of the WFM enlisted the IWW's help to shut down labour "sharks" who were flooding the area with unemployed workers.[11]

Support for the IWW increased when other unions, such as the United Mine Workers of America, turned in more conservative directions. As early as 1907, B.C. miners organized into the UMWA's District 18 announced they were "ready to start the propaganda for the IWW." This agitation culminated in the attempt in 1912 to break away from the United Mine Workers. Led by Wobbly miners, this serious rank and file movement was defeated by an alliance of socialists and UMWA loyalists, but the IWW managed to exact some changes and concessions. In the dramatic coal miners' strikes on Vancouver Island in 1912-14, the Miners' Liberation League was influenced greatly by the IWW, and a Wobbly was elected president of the League in 1913. Wobblies helped guide the strikes, and IWW tactics such as parades and direct action were used, while the union's call for a general strike was greeted enthusiastically. Only the refusal of the Vancouver Trades and Labor Council to support such a strike prevented it from taking place.[12]

The IWW's drives in the logging industry ran a parallel course to those in mining. By October 1907, Wobblies were active in Cranbrook, and late in 1909, IWW Lumber Workers' Local 45 was established in Vancouver. Its members went throughout the province organizing and working in the camps. Conditions in the lumber industry were uniformly dreadful, and one Wobbly's report described them with anger and humour:

> The Canadian Western Lumber Co., camp 7, Courtenay. The conditions of the camp: the oats are bum; plenty of slave drivers; in fact, the collar of your shirt is worn out in a few days, the stares from the drivers are so piercing. "Whoop her up boys, or hike." Bunk house fair. Monthly payment discount on checks; 50 cents for the use of stable for first month; wages from $3 to $6.50. Hospital fee $1.00. This entitles the slaves to the slaughter house and the services of a second-class butcher. For further information, I will refer you to a cock-eyed, caloused-brained stick of bobo, the bull cook second in command. Yours for Industrial Unionism, C. Nelson.[13]

Wobbly organizing drives went from Port Alberni to the Lower Mainland to the Kootenays. In Phoenix, John Riordan penned a poem for the timber beasts:

> When you chance to hit a strange burg,
> And you're absolutely broke,
> You're feeling rather hungry
> And there's nothing in your poke;
> You don't look up a preacher,

And the police you're sure to shun,
For no matter how you've rustled
They will spot you for a bum.

Your belt is getting very slack,
And you're about all in;
With the togs that you're arrayed in
Your chance is mighty thin.
For all to you are strangers,
And you've travelled from afar,
So in you drop to interview
The man behind the bar.

You take a glance around the room,
Some familiar face to see;
A gang of husky lumber jacks
Are out upon a spree.
They seem to understand your plight
As you saunter from the street,
And after asking you to drink,
They invite you out to eat

You're welcome to your share with them
While a single dime they've got,
So in the morning bright and early
With the gang you've cast your lot.
Back to the lumber woods once more
With the bunch you're on the tramp,
Till you've landed near the river
In a horrid lumber camp.

You make great resolutions
When your labor there begins.
Never again to taste or handle
Whiskey, beer or gin.
But labor all the winter long,
Until the good old summer-time,
Then hoist your bundle on your back
And hike it down the line.[14]

The loggers' union was small but militant. In Port Alberni, camp workers led by the Frenettes went on strike in 1911 to protest the trial of the McNamaras, two AFL activists who dynamited a Los Angeles newspaper building that was being built by non-union labour. In Vancouver, the local helped raise money for the New Bedford, Massachusetts textile strike and sent support to the McNamaras, whose case had become a *cause célèbre* for labour and the left.[15]

The local opposed attempts of employers to buy off workers with small reforms, and rejected measures that did not come from the working class. It bitterly denounced a provincial bill that called for health inspections of camps, pointing out that the bill was unopposed by bosses because they knew "they could get more work out of the men if better sanitary conditions were had. If the master ever discovers that more work can be accomplished with dirt, the same reasoning will apply and a 'BILL' will pass allowing lots of dirt." The writer concluded that the workers should instead fight for the eight-hour day, for then they would have "lots of time to keep nice and clean." Similarly, the local railed against a proposal from the Pacific Coast Loggers' Association, an "industrial union of slave drivers," to establish a government home for retired loggers. The union maintained that the welfare of the loggers should not depend on the state, for if the robbery by the bosses was ended, workers would "not need to be an object of charity." Instead, it reasoned, the Industrial Workers of the World would "put overalls on every capitalist in the country. To hell with their gifts."[16]

But attempts to organize loggers were largely unsuccessful, as were all attempts until the International Woodworkers of America, taking advantage of PC 1003, the Canadian government's war-time order-in-council which paved the way for large-scale organizing drives by unions, could win out in the 1940s. Accounts of the IWW obtaining the eight-hour day in the woods by simply blowing the whistle and heading back to camp after eight hours may be accurate in the United States, but there is no evidence to suggest that the tactic was used in B.C.. Organizing was difficult, for bosses could effectively keep agitators out of the camps. Alex Ferguson, Wobbly organizer in the 1920s, recalled that knapsacks and bindles were routinely searched as workers came to camp. Dedicated members often beat the searches, though, by picking up religious pamphlets in the city and hiding the union literature among their pages. Suspicious bosses "wouldn't mind a religious nut in camp," and once past inspection, the pie in the sky pamphlets could be dumped.[17]

But if the IWW disappeared as a formal organization in the woods in the 1910s, IWW delegates continued to spread their message of solidarity and education. As Gordon Hak points out in his Ph.D. thesis, individual members continued to "haunt" the logging camps, and Wobblies rose to prominence with the formation of the Lumber Workers' Industrial Union in 1919. IWW members continually challenged the more conservative leaders of the LWIU and pushed them to take more radical, militant stances. Ernest Winch, leader of the Lumber Workers, spent much of his time fighting off the syndicalists, and was pressured to "tacitly adopt IWW positions" at the 1920 convention.[18]

With the collapse of the LWIU in the early twenties, IWW locals were created to fill its place. The union established branches in Prince George, Vancouver, and Cranbrook in 1923, and organized in earnest. On 1 January 1924, workers in Lumberton, near Cranbrook, handed the B.C. Spruce Mills company "a New Year's gift in the shape of a walkout." The walkout was initially called to protest discrimination against an IWW member, but it soon spread to other camps and collected other grievances. The strikers demanded an eight-hour day, a daily wage of four dollars, an end to mail censorship, and no further discrimination against IWW members. In addition, the loggers demanded the release of all class war prisoners held in the United States, a universal demand of IWW locals at that time. Soon nearly a thousand loggers had stopped work, and the union rented houses to feed and shelter them. On 10 January, 350 workers employed by the Columbia River Company in Donald, B.C., put down their tools and hopped a train for Golden, about seventeen miles away. The men used the Columbia Hotel as a meeting hall, and shut down the liquor store and bootleggers to ensure peace and discipline.

The strike was widely supported by the merchants in the area. One donated sixty blankets, another a side of beef; the Wentworth Hotel in Cranbrook gave the IWW the use of its huge kitchen in return for the cost of the electric bill. People took in strikers as boarders and gave them food, while the union raised money to pay for those who were broke. When the employers brought in scabs, some from as far away as Winnipeg, union workers sent out pickets to convince them to join the strike, and many did. Flying picket squads, composed of "old-time lumberjacks who know all the old trails and who are not afraid of anything," traveled to remote camps to bring them out on the strike. Money poured in from IWW locals in Canada and the U.S. So effective was the shut-down that the Calgary and Vancouver Boards of Trade called upon the federal government to outlaw the IWW and to forbid its members from entering Canada. Immigration authorities were sent from Calgary to harass Wobblies and find cause to deport them, while the B.C. Department of Labour sent in the deputy minister, J.D. McNiven, to settle the strike. More effective than his efforts, however, were an anti-picketing injunction that forbade strikers to even discuss the strike with others, and the beginning of good weather. With the melting of the snow needed to sleigh out timber, logging would soon be curtailed, and strikers would be unable to put much real pressure on the employers. This at least was the rationale given by the union, and on 2 March, the loggers voted to continue the pressure "on the job," a veiled reference to sabotage, slow-downs, and similar tactics. Since none of the demands were won, and little else happened in subsequent months, it is fair to conclude that despite the heroic effort, the union was unable to exert enough pressure. The call to fight again another day was more than bravado, but it signalled defeat, not victory. The Mountain Lumber Manufacturers' Association soon instigated a black list to prevent any action on the job. The association warned its members that

> every effort should be made to prevent the IWW or their
> sympathizers obtaining a foothold in your operations. There
> is only one way to prevent this, and that is by destroying
> the root of the trouble—i.e., get rid of the agitators,
> delegates and in general the trouble makers. Eliminate them
> as far as possible before they enter your employ, by keeping
> a close check on all new men seeking employment."

The warning was accompanied by a list of names, and association members were urged to fire those who appeared on it and to add names and information so a revised list could be issued.[19]

In cities and towns, where most B.C. workers lived, the IWW formed mixed locals of general labourers. In Vancouver, the Lumber Handlers' Local 526 and Mixed Local 322 had organized nearly two hundred workers by March 1907. The locals sent telegrams of support during the famous Moyer, Haywood, and Pettibone murder trial in Idaho, and condemned the "proceeding of the capitalist class as perpetrating a worse condition than exists in barbarous Russia." In April of the same year, the locals supported a Vancouver strike of AFL painters and carpenters, and resolved that no IWW member would work in the building trades industry. The locals went so far as to expel one member who refused to join the boycott.[20] Later in the year, two Wobbly organizers who would later figure importantly in the union came to Vancouver. Joseph Ettor, who would help organize the famous Lawrence textile strike of 1912, organized an Italian local and applied for a charter for a general teamsters' local. In the fall of 1907, John H. Walsh helped organize a strike of lumber handlers in Vancouver. Walsh would later lead the famous "overalls brigade" from Spokane to the 1908 IWW convention in Chicago to help orchestrate the purging of Daniel DeLeon and the political faction from the union. He was also the first to use songs as an organizing tool, and was the pioneer behind the Wobblies' little red song book. The local of lumber handlers was composed of men from eighteen nationalities, and had already won two small strikes, one a protest against the use of deepwater sailors on the docks, the other a fight to increase wages and decrease hours. On 1 October 1907, the local was locked out by stevedores in an attempt to cut wages from 40 cents an hour to 35 and increase the hours of work from nine to ten. The union held out for a month, but when police prevented picketing and helped scabs to cross, the members voted to return to work at 40 cents an hour and a ten-hour day. Though the strike was viewed as a loss, Walsh pointed out proudly that "all our boys stood steadfast," and that the decision to return to work and keep the union intact for a winter organizing drive was made by the entire local unanimously.[21] In November, a Russian-language branch was organized in the city; one of its members was a former member of the Imperial Duma. The locals shared a headquarters that consisted of a meeting hall, a smoking and "rag-chewing room," and a large reading room. Weekly propaganda meetings were held, and the union had a small library in which "nearly every Socialist and revolutionary paper of the world" could be found.[22]

In 1910, Vancouver Wobblies helped lead a strike of Italian excavators for an eight-hour day and engineered a short strike of labourers who were constructing the city's race track. The city's Wobblies worked to put the union on a more solid footing by calling for a convention of all Pacific Coast locals. In order to produce and distribute more literature, fund and organize speaking tours, and promote better co-operation and solidarity, they reasoned, a tighter network had to be created. Even with the existing loose ties, the Vancouver locals managed to bring in speakers such as Lucy Parsons, William Haywood, Joe Ettor, and Elizabeth Gurley Flynn. The locals supported the AFL's general strike in the building trades in 1911, and held meetings and raised money for the effort. Several Wobblies left town rather than add to the growing army of unemployed. One, George Drogowicz, had been a member for only eight days when he rode the rails to the United States. His body was found outside Seattle on 25 June, hit by a train on the North Pacific tracks. Meanwhile, AFL bricklayers refused to join the strike and kept working.[23]

Victoria was home to a number of IWW locals. Number 44, with Alice Harling as secretary, was established by the summer of 1909. In May 1911, the union filled the Crystal Theatre to its capacity of 580 to call for a general strike to free the McNamaras. In the winter of that year, the IWW joined with the SPC to commemorate the anniversary of the murder of Spanish educator and radical Jose Ferrer. While the branch remained critical of the SPC and the AFL, it had friendly relations with them and often supported their rallies and strikes. In November 1911, Wobblies marched with AFL members to support union musicians who had been replaced by non-union ones at the Empress Hotel. While pointing out that the chairman of the parade was a union official who was also a "noted heeler for the Conservative party," the IWW concluded that it was not "wise to altogether knock on such occasions, but to march and strike with craft unions and endeavor to pave the way for the ONE BIG UNION idea, class organization, and solidarity of the working class."[24]

In April 1912, Victoria's IWW organizers were surprised to find three hundred "Greeks, Italians, Americans, Canucks, and colored men" show up at the union hall and ask to join up. Employed by the Canadian Mineral Rubber Company to pave the city streets, the men were paid $2.75 a day—25 cents less than the city's minimum scale. A black man was elected chairman of the strike committee, and together with the IWW, the workers put forward a demand for a 25-cent raise, full-time work, and a ban on overtime. The spontaneous uprising was chaotic, for the workers had little idea how to picket. Several were arrested and sentenced to a month in jail; others were beaten. In a show of solidarity, the SPC, the Social Democratic Party, and the Victoria Trades and Labor Council held joint meetings to support and raise money for the IWW strikers. The strike was over by early May, with no reports of victory, but IWW members promised that "the agitation still goes on."[25]

Less than a year later, a new local, the Building Workers' Industrial Union, was formed in the city. The local was, in the words of the IWW, the "natural outcome of repeated failures on the part of the AF of L to force the master to grant a raise in wages. All indications point to the gradual dissolution of the craft union and the construction of the modern industrial union on class lines." Despite this optimistic assessment, and the subsequent arrest of two Wobblies for stickering light poles, little came from this local. In May 1914, local 53 voted to disband. The seven members present, including George Hardy, sent the local's library to the IWW branch in Sydney, Australia, and the Wobbly presence in Victoria effectively ended, a victim of the pre-war downturn in the economy that drove many workers to seek opportunities elsewhere.[26]

Locals of the IWW were formed in Nelson soon after 1905. By late 1910, the Wobblies made up the largest union in the city, and soon won an eight-hour day and higher wages for city workers. The success of the IWW agitation attracted many AFL workers: half of the members of the Carpenters' union and the Electrical Workers also carried the little red card.[27]

The Prince Rupert labourers' local was the most successful. In April 1909, Patrick Daly, a former WFM member, helped organize railway construction workers into an IWW branch, and immediately launched a strike against the Grand Trunk Pacific railway. The strike did little to increase wages or better conditions, but over four hundred men joined the union and the IWW was established as a force to be reckoned with. In June, 123 men walked off a sewer construction site and appealed to the union for help. The contractor was forced out of business, and when the municipality took over the job, it was compelled to pay the union rate. The IWW office became the hiring hall for most of Prince Rupert's labourers, and by October IWW longshoremen controlled the local waterfront.[28] In 1911, the local helped establish the Prince Rupert Industrial Association, a broadly-based union of construction workers. The association soon raised the going rate from $3.00 per eight-hour day to $3.60, but some private contractors refused to raise wages. On 1 March, the association voted to strike to win the higher rate for all workers. At first the strike was limited to private contractors, but as scabs were imported from Vancouver, city workers joined in. On 6 April, a parade of several hundred workers marched through Prince Rupert to Kelly's Cut. Special police hired by the contractors shot four of the strikers and ransacked the union hall. More than fifty workers were arrested on charges ranging from unlawful assembly to attempted murder, and craft union workers were hired to build a bull pen to hold the men. Fifteen men were later tried in Victoria: while some were acquitted, one was sentenced to three years, five to two years, three to one year, and one to six months, though all were released in less than a year. The members of the PRIA voted to join the Wobblies *en masse*, and over one thousand men were issued red cards. One union activist wrote "The Battle of Kelly's Cut" to commemorate the strike:

> Come all you workers if you want to hear,
> I will tell you a story of a great pioneer.
> Prince Rupert is the pioneer's name;
> The way she started she won her fame.
>
> Her streets were of plank, her people of pluck,
> Who had gathered on the townsite
> To try their luck.
>
> The railroad was coming and that we knew.
> Our hopes were many, but our dollars few.
> A port was to open to world wide trade.
> A lot then held was a fortune made.
>
> Some had not lot, and had no coin;
> So a pick and shovel they had to join.
> Wages were small and the rain did pour;
> To feed our families we had to get more.
>
> In a little Church up on the hill,
> A union was formed that is remembered still.
> Prince Rupert Industrial Association was the union's name:
> At the Kelly Cut Battle it won its fame.
>
> Some members were from Sweden and some came from
>   Spain.
> Others came from Serbia and the State of Maine;
> Ireland had her quota, England had a few;
> Scotland had her number and Italy too.

In that union we had some men,
Who could coin you a nickel from an old hair pin.
All went well that day
When from a parade a few did stray
To a Scabby Spot along the way.

Within a minute a battle did start
And as a union, all took part.
Some threw rocks, others had a gun;
Believe me or not, it was no fun.

All nations were at war; police came running
And arrested quite a few.
A bullpen was built; our boys placed inside.
A court then was held and many took a ride.
To the pen they were sentenced—up to seven years;
If you had a heart it would drive you to tears.

The result of that battle never will die,
In the hearts of Oldtimers it still does lie.
A wage scale was established and there did remain,
Until the workers moved and revised it again.
A boycott was established and soon put on the bum
Was the man who had the store and was handy with the
    gun.

So Boys, keep up your courage,
Though it is no fun;
You will never win the battle
If you turn and run.[29]

But the IWW's greatest successes were among the upwards of
8,000 railway navvies who worked on the Canadian Northern
and Grand Trunk Pacific lines and electrified the province with
their strike. The drives to organize the construction workers
meant that the Wobblies were able to move from the periphery to
the very heart of the province's economy. Organizers were active
on the western end of the GTP in 1909, and reports came in from
other areas in the province. One such report, from Keremeos on
the Great Northern line, was typical:

> The sharks are shipping to Keremeos, B.C. This is station
> work by small gunny-sack contractors. Fee $1, and you must
> take the stage from 5 to 10 miles after arriving at Keremeos
> Valley. Wages $2.25 to $2.50. Discount, and hard to beat
> back on the railroad. The sharks ask $1.50 for a division.
> Everybody says this is a rotten lay-out. Keep away.[30]

Organizing began in earnest in the summer of 1911. By August, Carl Berglund had put together a "propaganda club" of eight hundred men at Spence's Bridge on the CN line and reported that the men were waiting for an IWW organizer so a union local could be formally established. Organizers were busy at Lytton, a few miles south, as well. J.S. Biscay was sent from Vancouver to bring in the workers to the IWW, and signed up over six hundred in his first few weeks on the job. The organizer was excited by the progress, and wrote that the "bunch here are so enthusiastic that they won't stand for a non-union man around the camps.... I never saw a finer example of solidarity than has been manifest here. The boys simply won't stand for any foolishness." By October, Biscay had lined up over 1500 in the union, and plans were made to build a headquarters in Lytton. Despite initial interference from the police, regular meetings were held in the town and the agitation continued.[31]

Contractors were first skeptical about the prospects for the union's success. But the efforts of Biscay and others soon started them into action. On 22 September, at a camp fifteen miles from Savona, police and company thugs beat and kidnapped Biscay. When his valise was later searched, a gun was found, and the Wobbly was charged with "being a dangerous character and a menace to public safety." Held in the Kamloops jail for over a month, Biscay was finally found not guilty by a jury and released. By this time, the union had grown to over three thousand members.[32]

The Wobbly penchant for poetry continued during the drive. An allegory entitled "It Pays to Kick" was written by "A Jobite on the Canadian Northern":

> There lived two frogs, so I am told,
> In a quiet wayside pool;
> One of those frogs was a darn big frog;
> The other frog was a fool.
>
> Now a farmer man with a big milk can,
> Was wont to pass that way;
> And he used to stop and add a drop
> Of the Agua, so they say.
>
> It happened one morn in the early dawn,
> When the farmer's sight was dim,
> He scooped those frogs in the water he dipped,
> Which same was a joke on him.

The fool frog sank in the swishing tank,
As the farmer bumped to town.
But the smart frog flew like a tugboat screw,
And swore he'd never go down.

So he kicked and splashed and spluttered and thrashed,
He kept on top through all.
And he churned that milk in first class shape,
Into a nice large butter ball.

Now when the farmer got into town
And opened the can, there lay
The fool frog drowned.
But hale and sound, the KICKER; he flopped away.

Moral:
Don't waste your life in endless strife,
But let this teaching stick.
You'll find, old man, in the world's big can
It sometimes pays to KICK.[33]

On 27 March 1912, the workers on the CN line did kick. IWW members at Nelson and Benson's camp number four, a few miles from Lytton, walked out to protest wages and sanitary conditions. A meeting was held in the town to draw up a list of demands and elect strike committees. Soon over four thousand men from Hope and Kamloops were out on strike. The men built their own camps, started commissaries, and set up "courts" to police the camps. Infractions of the rules were punished by sentences such as "go and cut ten big armsful of firewood," "carry ten coal-oil cans full of water for the camp cooks," or "help the cooks for one day." The men were restricted to two drinks of liquor a day, and local saloon keepers were warned that all liquor would be thrown out if the rule was broken. One newspaper reporter observed that the "strike seems to have acted like a wave of reform," and that the Yale camp resembled a "miniature republic run on Socialistic lines, and it must be admitted that so far it has been run successfully."[34]

In May, the VTLC received an appeal for help from the workers, but before sending aid, the council had a member investigate the conditions. He reported that they were as bad as the Wobblies had alleged:

The men live in shacks without floor or windows. . . . Owing to the overcrowding and lack of ventilation, the air became

so foul nights that it was not an uncommon occurrence for
the men to arise in the morning too sick to work. . . . [I]n one
camp, a toilet was placed so that the refuse was discharged
in the river immediately upstream from the place where
water was drawn for cooking purposes.

The report encouraged the VTLC to give some financial support
to the strikers, and the council issued a call to its affiliates for
money. In June, its paper, the *B.C. Federationist*, became the
official strike bulletin for the tie-up. [35]

In the camps, the strike committees arranged talks on industrial unionism "and other working class matters, not only from
the view point of the immediate strike, but also as to the future."[36]
Joe Hill, the famous IWW songwriter and martyr, arrived in Yale
ten days after the strike broke out and wrote several songs. The
only one which has survived intact is "Where the Fraser River
Flows," written to the tune of "Where the River Shannon Flows":

Fellow workers, pay attention to what I'm going to mention,
For it is the fixed intention of the Workers of the World,
And I hope you'll all be ready, true-hearted, brave and
    steady,
To gather round our standard when the Red Flag is
    unfurled.

Chorus:

Where the Fraser River flows, each fellow worker knows
They have bullied and oppressed us, but still our union
    grows;
And we're going to find a way boys, for shorter hours and
    better pay, boys,
We're going to win the day boys, where the Fraser River
    flows.

Now these gunny sack contractors have all been dirty actors;
They're not our benefactors, each fellow workers knows.
So we've got to stick together in fine or dirty weather,
And we will show no white feather where the Fraser River
    flows.

Now the boss the law is stretching, bulls and pimps he's
    fetching,
And they are a fine collection, as Jesus only knows.
But why their mother reared them, and why the devil
    spared them,

> Are questions we can't answer where the Fraser River
> flows.[37]

Louis Moreau, who had been a camp delegate during the strike, later remembered the effect the songs had:

> The Wobblies drove those contractors nuts. One day Martin [a contractor] came by our camp at Yale annex and started to talk to a bunch of Swedes that were sitting alongside of the road. When the groaning brigade, our singing sextet, started to sing the song Joe had made for him, Martin tore his hair and swore he'd get us.[38]

The IWW made Martin and other contractors do more than just pull their hair. By 2 April, they had met with Premier Richard McBride and asked for militia troops to end the strike; while the premier demurred on the question of military aid, he did dispatch special constables and allowed the companies to swear in and arm foremen as constables. The men were sent on the pretext that order needed to be restored, in spite of police reports that the level of violence and disorderly conduct had actually gone down during the strike. Provincial health inspectors were sent to close the workers' camps, even though they were cleaner than the CN camps. Strikers were harassed by police and company thugs: one man was shot in the leg by a company constable, while another was run down by a train.[39]

During the third week of April, the police intensified their campaign against the strike. The men were ordered to return to work, and when they refused, armed constables entered the camps and ousted them at gunpoint. Several camps were destroyed and sweeping arrests were made. By June, nearly three hundred men were imprisoned on charges ranging from vagrancy to inciting to murder, and many more were driven from the area. Immigration authorities kept IWW men from entering the area, but they eased restrictions for men willing to scab. Donald Mann, one of the magnates of the CN, used his influence to change immigration regulations to facilitate the importation of navvies from the United States, and it became more difficult to keep scabs out. The Wobblies' "1,000 mile picket line," which had union members picketing employment offices in Vancouver, Seattle, Tacoma, Minneapolis, and San Francisco to curtail the hiring of scabs, began to falter. An IWW request for arbitration under the

Industrial Disputes Investigation Act was refused by the federal government and the railways, thus supporting the Wobbly contention that the state was not a friend to labour.[40]

On 20 July, workers on the Grand Trunk Pacific line from Prince Rupert to Edmonton struck for demands similar to those of the CN workers. The strike bulletin published a grim joke which reflected the conditions:

> Undertaker: I've advertised for an assistant. Have you any experience at funerals?
> Applicant: I should say so! I was doctor in a railroad construction camp for three years.[41]

Though both strikes continued into the winter, work had resumed on the CN line by July and the GTP line by September. The CN strike was never officially called off, but in January 1913, the Prince Rupert local declared the GTP strike over. The local noted that the strikers had forced the federal government to promise to enforce sanitary regulations and that the strike "really gained more than the strikers had hoped for."[42]

Organizers continued their work on the railways. In February 1913, several men struck the Kettle Valley line near Naramata in a short-lived attempt to improve conditions. Workers struck again in April, and in May four hundred navvies went out. But it was too difficult to feed and house the men, and the strike was called off a week later, though some concessions were granted.[43]

Railway contractors had learned from the earlier strikes and organizers found it increasingly difficult to agitate. Wobblies were run out of town, arrested, and beaten. Joseph Ettor was deported, and other IWW men were driven out of camps. One writer described the lengths to which contractors would go:

> To show how scared the thieving railroad contractors are, we mention the fact that a crippled man, who was unable to work, went up to Tuohey's camp on the North Thompson to beg a few dimes and was run out of the place because the gunnysackers thought he was an IWW organizer in disguise. Just wait until we really get into action![44]

Despite this bold challenge, the IWW was unable to repeat the success of 1912. Indeed, the railway strikes remained the highwater mark of the union's activities in B.C.. Continued employer hostility, wartime repression, and the end of the railway boom all played a part in the decline of IWW, as they did in the decline of all left-wing groups at the time. Wobblies faced another challenge, however, that came from their erstwhile allies on the left. It is hard to assess the damage caused by factionalism in B.C., but as the following chapter shows, it played a role in the eventual eclipse of the IWW. In addition, the closer examination of the different ideologies, strategies, and personalities in the B.C. labour and left movements highlights their evolution into the business unionism and social democracy of today.

Notes for Chapter 2

1. I share G.S. Kealey's reservations over the characterization of the historiographical debate as "generational," but use the concept here as a convenient shorthand. Kealey's point is in "Labour and Working-Class History in Canada: Prospects in the 1900s," *Labour/Le Travailleur* 7 (Spring 1981), p. 93. Bryan Palmer formulated the argument in "Working-Class Canada: Recent Historical Writing," *Queen's Quarterly* Volume 86, Number 4 (Winter 79/80). For the debate between the generations, see, for example, Palmer's introduction to *A Culture in Conflict*; Robert Sweeny, "Theory, Method, and Sources: The Search for Historical Logic," paper presented at the Workshop on Regional History, Victoria, February 1986; Terry Morley, "Canada and the Romantic Left," *Queen's Quarterly* Volume 86, Number 1 (Spring 1979); Kenneth McNaught, "E.P. Thompson vs Harold Logan: Writing About Labour and the Left in the 1970s," *Canadian Historical Review*, Volume 62, Number 2 (June 1981); David Bercuson, "Through the Looking Glass of Culture," *Labour/Le Travailleur* 7 (Spring 1981); Palmer, "Modernizing History," *Bulletin of the Committee on Canadian Labour History* 2 (Autumn 1976) and Michael Katz, "Reply," ibid.; Daniel Drache, "The Formation and Fragmentation of the Canadian Working Class: 1820-1920," *Studies in Political Economy* 15 (Fall 1984); Palmer, "Listening to History Rather Than Historians: Reflections on Working Class History," *Studies in Political Economy* 20 (Summer 1986). The E.P. Thompson quote on the Parsons/Smelser school is in *The Making of the English Working Class*. Middlesex: Penguin Books, revised edition 1968, p. 11. Pritchard is cited in Bercuson, *Fools and Wise Men: The Rise and Fall of the One Big Union*. Toronto: McGraw-Hill Ryerson, 1978, p. xix. His statement regarding mining safety appears in *Fools and Wise Men*, p. 2; see also Bercuson, "Labour Radicalism and the Western Industrial Frontier, 1897-1919," in *B.C. Historical Readings*. Vancouver: Douglas and McIntyre, 1981, W. Peter Ward and Robert A.J. McDonald, editors, pp. 451-473.

2. Allen Seager, "Socialists and Workers: the Western Canadian Coal Miners, 1900-21," *Labour/Le Travail* 16 (Fall, 1985) p. 25.

3. See, for example, Paul Phillips, *No Power Greater: A Century of Labour*

in B.C.. Vancouver: B.C. Federation of Labour/Boag Foundation, 1967;
Martin Robin, *The Rush for Spoils: The Company Province, 1871-1933.*
Toronto: McClelland and Stewart, 1972; Phillips, "The National Policy
and the Development of the Western Canadian Labour Movement," in
Prairie Perspective 2. Toronto: Holt, Rhinehart, and Winston, 1973, A.W.
Rasporich and H.C. Klassen, editors; Margaret Ormsby, *British
Columbia: A History.* Toronto: Macmillan, 1958, pp. 327-372.

4. Robert A.J. McDonald, "Working Class Vancouver, 1886-1914:
Urbanism and Class in British Columbia." *B.C. Studies* 69-70
(Spring-Summer 1986) pp. 33-69.

5. A. Ross McCormack, *Reformers, Rebels, and Revolutionaries: The Western
Canadian Radical Movement, 1899-1919.* Toronto: University of Toronto
Press, 1979, p. 17.

6. Kenneth McNaught, *The Pelican History of Canada.* Middlesex:
Penguin Books, 1976; J.L. Finlay and D.N. Sprague, *The Structure of
Canadian History.* Scarborough: Prentice-Hall, second edition, 1984; J.L.
Granatstein *et al., Twentieth Century Canada.* Toronto: McGraw
Hill-Ryerson, 1983. This error has been corrected in the second edition.
Desmond Morton with Terry Copp, *Working People: An Illustrated History
of the Canadian Labour Movement.* Ottawa: Deneau Publishers, 1984, revised
edition, p. 96; McCormack, p. 98-117; Ralph Allen, *Ordeal By Fire:
Canada 1910-1945.* Garden City: Doubleday, 1961, pp. 175-177; Phillips,
No Power Greater, pp. 158, 52; Jack Scott, *Plunderbund and Proletariat: A
History of the IWW in B.C..* Vancouver: New Star Books, 1975

7. McCormack, p. 99; Phillips, *No Power Greater,* p. 46; *IUB,* 10
August, 20 April, 10 October 1907.

8. *IW,* 8 April 1909. For the etymology of the word "Wobbly," see *The
Nation,* 5 September 1923, p. 242. Stewart Holbrook, in *American Mercury,*
Volume 7, January 1926, p. 62, claims the term was similarly coined in
Saskatchewan in 1914 during the construction of the CNR. H.L.
Mencken, in *The American Language,* suggests that this etymology is
"unlikely," but offers no other. In fact, no other explanation has ever
been accepted. Fred Thompson, in the official IWW history, p. 67,
suggests that the term may have come from the "wobble saw," a circular
saw mounted askew so that it cut a groove wider than the thickness of
the blade—an interesting metaphor for the union. In his fictional account
of the Centralia events, *Dead March.* Willimantic, Connecticut: Curbstone
Press, 1980, p. 8, Tom Churchill cites a Wobbly who gives the "wobble
saw" derivation but claims it was a saw that "cut in both directions."
Neither Dubofsky nor Kornbluh gives an etymology. Philip Foner, in
Fellow Workers, gives the Chinese restaurant theory, and cites *Solidarity,* 1
November 1913, for the source. I was unable to find such an account in
that issue, though I did find there a letter from John E. Nordquist of Des
Moines, Iowa, that reads, in part, "The 'wobbly' cause is booming in
this boasted 'City of Certainties' now....The membership is growing
rapidly and we are looking for a larger hall to accommodate the
'Wobbies' [sic]." The *Oxford English Dictionary Supplement* holds that the
etymology is unknown, and gives its earliest use as 5 April 1913, in
Miners Magazine. Merriam Webster's *Third International Dictionary* states
that the origin is "unknown," as does Eric Partridge in *A Dictionary of*

Slang and Unconventional English. In a letter to the author, dated 31 January 1989, Craig M. Carver, managing editor of the *Dictionary of American Regional English*, states that the Chinese restaurateur version is not given "much credence...because the story is simply unverifiable." Those with a scientific bent must conclude that the etymology is unknown; romantics may choose to stick with Downing.

9. See Star Rosenthal, "Union Maids: Organized Women Workers in Vancouver 1900-1915," *B.C. Studies* 41 (Spring 1979), pp. 36-55, for the attitude of the IWW to women. Details on Edith Frenette may be found in Elizabeth Gurley Flynn, *The Rebel Girl: An Autobiography—My First Life (1906-26).* New York: International Publishers, 1971, pp. 104, 108, 221; and in Foner, *The IWW*, pp. 525, 527, 529. The story of Stella Frenette and the organizing in Port Alberni is in *IW*, 3 August 1911, 2 November 1911, 18 April 1912. The names of women who headed the Victoria local are in *IW* 16 August 1909 and 29 December 1910; I could find no other details about them.

10. *Founding Convention*, p. 297; Brissenden, p. 137; Foner, *The IWW*, p. 71; Thompson, pp. 23, 25; McCormack, p. 100; *IUB*, 30 March, 13 July, 5 October, 30 November 1907. For the recent posthumous pardon of Smith and Preston, see *IW*, June 1987.

11. *IUB*, 5 October 1907; *IW*, 12 August 1909, 7 October 1909.

12. *IUB*, 23 November 1907; McCormack, pp. 113-115; Phillips, *No Power Greater*, p. 60.

13. McCormack, p. 101; *IUB*, 12 October 1907; *IW*, 30 April, 2 November 1910.

14. *IW*, 29 December 1910.

15. Gordon Hak, "On the Fringes: Capital and Labour in the Forest Economies of the Port Alberni and Prince George Districts, British Columbia, 1910-1939." Ph.D. dissertation, Simon Fraser University, 1986, pp. 172-173; *IW*, 25 June 1910, 6 July, 26 October, 2 November 1911.

16. *IW*, 2 February, 13 July 1911.

17. Alex Ferguson, interview with author, Vancouver, February 1976.

18. Hak, pp. 156, 270; see Bercuson, *Fools and Wise Men*, pp. 165-66, for the pressure on Winch; Vancouver *Sun*, 22 February 1924; Victoria *Colonist*, 12 February, 8 February, 7 February 1924; Victoria *Times*, 23 January 1924; *Canadian Labour Gazette*, 1924, pp. 108, 219, 294.

19. *IW*, 2 January, 9 January, 12 January, 16 January, 23 January, 2 February, 5 March, 8 March, 12 March 1924; Vancouver *Sun*, 22 February 1924; Victoria *Colonist*, 7 February, 8 February, 12 February 1924; *Canada Labour Gazette*, 1924, pp. 108, 219, 294. The letter appears in the RCMP IWW file, Item 95, dated 14 March 1924, copy in the author's possession; the list of names, unfortunately, has been deleted.

20. *IUB*, 23 March, 20 April, 27 April, 4 May 1907.

21. *IUB*, 2 November, 9 November 1907; 2 May 1908.

22. *IUB*, 7 December 1907.

23. *IW*, 30 July, 21 May, 15 December 1910; 8 June, 15 June, 22 June, 29 June, 6 July, 13 July, 20 July 1911.

24. *IW*, 26 August 1909, 25 May 1911, 7 December 1911.

25. *IW*, 18 April, 9 May 1912.

26. *IW*, 17 April, 24 April 1913; *Solidarity*, 20 June 1914; George Hardy, *Those Stormy Years: Memories of the Fight for Freedom on Five Continents*. London: Lawrence and Wishart, 1956, pp. 56-57. Hardy states that the outbreak of World War One was responsible for the exodus of workers and Wobblies from B.C. His memory is a little faulty, for the Victoria branch shut down a few weeks before Archduke Ferdinand was assassinated in Sarajevo. No doubt he is correct to argue that the economic decline at that time was responsible.

27. *IW*, 29 December 1910; *B.C. Federationist*, 16 January 1914; Phillips, p. 55; Scott, p. 27.

28. *IW*, 15 April, 20 May, 24 June, 8 June, 15 June, 22 June, 29 June, 6 July, 17 October 1909.

29. *IW*, 6 April, 20 April, 27 April, 25 May, 29 June 1911; "Fighting for Labour: Four Decades of Work in British Columbia, 1910-1950." *Sound Heritage*, Volume 4, Number 4. Compiled by Patricia Wejr and Howie Smith, 1978, pp. 8-11.

30. *IW*, 16 September 1909.

31. *IW*, 17 August, 31 August, 14 September, 28 September 1911.

32. *IW*, 5 October, 12 October, 19 October, 2 November 1911.

33. *IW*, 4 January 1912.

34. *IW*, 4 April, 11 April 1912; Vancouver *Province*, 3 April 1912.

35. *IW*, 11 April 1912; *B.C. Federationist*, 22 June 1912; Phillips, *No Power Greater*, p. 53.

36. *IW*, 18 April 1912.

37. Gibbs M. Smith, *Joe Hill*. 1969. Reprint. Salt Lake City: Peregrine Smith Books, 1984, pp. 24-26; *IW*, 9 May 1912. The *IW* of 9 September 1909 defined a "gunnysack contractor" as "an exploiter of the proletariat having very little capital." In this case, it was a reference to the stationmen who often made little more than the navvies did.

38. Smith, p. 25.

39. Vancouver *Sun*, 3 April, 16 April 1912; *Province*, 2 April, 3 April 1912; McCormack, p. 109; *IW*, 18 April 1912.

40. *Sun*, 16 April, 17 April 1912; *IW*, 25 April, 1 May 1912; *Solidarity*, 4 May 1912; *IW*, 9 May, 16 May, 23 May, 30 May 1912; Thompson and Murfin, *The IWW: Its First Seventy Years*, pp. 65-66; Avery, *Dangerous Foreigners*, p. 55.

41. *IW*, 25 July, 5 September 1912.

42. Phillips, *No Power Greater*, p. 54; McCormack, p. 109; *IW*, 23 January 1913.

43. *IW*, 6 March, 24 April, 8 May 1913.

44. *IW*, 6 March, 27 March, 3 April, 13 March 1913; *Solidarity*, 15 March 1913; *IW*, 15 May 1913; *Solidarity*, 10 January 1914.

CHAPTER 3

Solidarity on Occasion

Despite constant calls for solidarity and unity, the labour movement in B.C. was often divided. Different tendencies, ideas, and activists fought over the best ways to advance labour's cause. The in-fighting was rarely a calm matter of reasoned debate. It reflected different ideologies, different programs, different world-views, and it often took place in the heat of battles with capital and the state. The direct action of the IWW interfered with the orderly electoral process desired by the SPC; rank and file militancy conflicted with the evolutionary designs of the international craft unions.

The Socialist Party of Canada was particularly hostile to the IWW. Less than two weeks after the founding convention of the IWW, the *Western Clarion*, the SPC's newspaper, assailed the new organization as a "living picture of a mental vacuity on the part of its parents." A week later, the paper denounced the Wobblies as "ignorant asses" and "gabblers," and suggested that the "Chicago affair will go down in history as the most ridiculous and impotent fiasco that ever happened in the name of labour."[1] Attacks on the union, ranging from bitter personal attacks to more reasoned attacks on its aims and tactics, appeared regularly in the paper. A few months after the 1912 free speech fight in Vancouver, the *Clarion* reprinted an article from the Los Angeles newspaper the *Citizen* which forcefully attacked the IWW, claiming that "the time is 'ripe and rotten ripe' for a complete showing up of the traitors who are exploiting the struggles of the workers and undermining the institutions erected at infinite sacrifice for their protection and advancement." In a later issue, the *Clarion* argued against direct action, claiming that only political action could free the working class. Decrying the IWW as an anarchist organization, the writer concluded that "if the IWW is not financed by the capitalist class, it ought to be!"[2]

During the CN strike, the Socialist Party commended the B.C.

local of the IWW for its conduct, but nonetheless went on to argue that the union was "so anarchistic, and therefore reactionary, as to clearly stamp it as an enemy of the peaceful and orderly process of the labor movement towards the overthrow of capital and the ending of wage servitude." This is a far cry from "the impossibilism" usually attributed to the party. Another article pointed out that while the strike had cost the IWW thirty thousand dollars, the "strikers had nothing but sore heads to show for it." The writer suggested that the money would have been better spent on the nomination fees of fifty Socialist Party candidates and used to "smother British Columbia with Socialist literature, and the results would be 10 or 15 working class representatives in Victoria."[3] Coming in the middle of the strike, such editorials were hardly designed to build solidarity.

Though its editorials were a little more restrained, the trade union movement also attacked Wobblies. The *Western Wage-Earner*, for example, attacked the IWW as disruptive and parasitic:

> In nearly every instance where the unorganized revolt
> against existing conditions and secure even a semblance of
> victory, a number of organizers appear on the scene in time
> to claim a victory for the Industrial Workers of the World,
> allegedly an Industrial union, but in reality nothing but a
> number of sharp fakirs who are able to temporarily enthuse
> the half-starved incredulous workers, thereby securing per-
> capita tax for a brief period. . . . Unlike the craft and industrial
> unions, this aggregation, better known as the Infant Wonder
> Workers, has no real mission, except the disruption of
> existing organizations, both industrial and political.[4]

The paper, representing the skilled trade unionist, often denounced the hoboes who were the organizing constituency of the IWW. In July 1909, it printed an article which asked, "What shall we do with the tramp?" The answer was blunt: "Let him continue to hit the grit. It is more healthful for him to tramp all over the country than to loaf in one town, and better for the town."[5] Another issue noted that New Westminster bartenders were being licensed and charged two dollars for the privilege, but that

> not a few of the men affected to believe that if a license is to
> be imposed it should be a large one, say $25. With a higher

license, they say, it would have a tendency to keep out
travelling "tramps," as they designate transients in the
trade, and improve the class of men in the business. It
would also, they claim, protect local men who live in the
city and have their homes and property here.[6]

The trade union paper also printed anecdotes that took swipes
at transient workers. In one, the "Tramp" goes up to a house and
speaks with the lady: "'Good morning, mum! Nice dog you have,
mum! What d'ye call him?' Lady of the House—'There's no need
to mention his name. He'll go to you without calling as soon as I
loose his chain.'"[7] In another, "Plodding Pete" asks, "'Is it true
dat yous is offering work to anybody that comes along?' 'Yep,'
replies farmer Corntassel, 'jes' take off your coat an'—' 'Not me,
I'm jes' a scout sent ahead by de other fellers to verify a terrible
rumour.'"[8]

The labour movement's blows were not limited to editorials
and anecdotes. Often the unions actively fought the IWW. In
1907, Wobbly organizer Joe Ettor complained of attempts of SPC
and VTLC stalwart Parm Pettipiece to raid the union:

> One of the characteristic methods of the AF of L in
> organizing is to try and take advantage of the work done by
> the IWW and reap where this organization has sown. This
> was attempted at Vancouver, B.C., by one Pettipiece, a
> counterfeit wearing the buttons of the SP and AF of L on
> his coat collar. The vigilance of Organizer Ettor and other
> IWW men, however, spoiled the game. Pettipiece has been
> challenged to debate the "difference," but it is a safe bet
> that he'll never show up. [9]

In the town of Nelson, the AFL went so far as to send in an
organizer to disrupt the unity of the movement and purge the
IWW. Believing that the strength of the revolutionary union
hindered the "natural development of the labor movement on the
economic and political fronts," George H. Hardy went in to
isolate the Wobblies and end the dual unionism that had "undermined" the internationals. Building on the local support for a
trade council, Hardy used the desire for solidarity to remove the
IWW. Though the union organized civic workers, teamsters, and
unskilled labourers, and though half of the AFL carpenters and
electrical workers carried Wobbly cards, Hardy manoeuvred to
prevent the IWW from attending the founding meetings of the

trade council. When others protested, he relied on a legalistic sleight of hand. Admitting that the Wobblies had organized many workers, and that the "unskilled trade would be an asset to the labor movement," Hardy maintained that the AFL charter granted to him to form the trade council "unfortunately excluded their membership. " Playing members off each other and dangling the carrot of AFL support, Hardy managed to split the IWW from the rest of the labour movement. This isolation had important ramifications for the union. Believing that they would continue to be outflanked in a straightforward competition with the AFL, Nelson Wobblies soon voted to form the first local of the Syndicalist League of North America. Formed by William Z. Foster, a former IWW member and later head of the American Communist Party, the League believed that the best course for revolutionaries was to abandon the dual unionism of the IWW and to join AFL unions. Once inside, syndicalists could "bore from within" and eventually turn the conservative unions into revolutionary ones. Unfortunately, revolutionaries fared no better inside the AFL than outside it. Two years after Hardy provoked Jack Johnstone into taking Nelson Wobblies into the League, there was "neither 'league,' AF of L, nor IWW there, in the lumber camps, or woods" of the area.[10]

The AFL leadership worked in other ways to hamper the IWW. By 1906, Samuel Gompers and his Canadian secretary-treasurer, Frank Morrison, were worried enough to send organizers to B.C. to compete with the Wobblies. Morrison funded organizing efforts in the Pacific Northwest with the avowed purpose of preventing the IWW from "secur[ing] the confidence and affiliation of the workers in those rapidly growing cities." John A. Flett, former Hamilton carpenter, former Knight of Labor, and the chief representative of Gompers in Canada, was shipped west to bolster the craft internationals and disrupt IWW drives. To counter the union's work in the lumber camps, the AFL and the VTLC agreed to begin organizing the timber beasts in 1912. The *B.C. Federationist* was quick to the attack. The paper suggested, accurately, that the IWW's logging union was little more than a remnant, then suggested rather less accurately that the money raised by the locals went straight into the pockets of their organizers. The *Industrial Worker* responded in kind, pointing out icily that the IWW had at least six times as many loggers signed up as the AFL did, despite the AFL's half-hearted attempts to organize the woods over the previous thirty years. The paper also noted that the "lowest wage paid to any AF of L organizer is as large and generally much larger than the highest paid to the IWW organizers."[11]

Gompers was quick to use the skills of the AFL's Pacific Northwest regional organizer to isolate the IWW. C.O. Young had been a Knight of Labor, but with its decline, he became a strong craft unionist. Working out of Spokane, he agitated against the IWW, and advised union members to be "cautious and conservative," and to run the unions on "strict business lines." Young undermined the IWW free speech fight in Missoula, and supported Spokane authorities for their repression and violence during a similar battle there. Canadian Wobblies denounced Young and his business unionism. Writing from Phoenix, B.C., one attacked the AFL agent as a "labor faker" who had sold out strikers in Blaine. He suggested that if Young would "get a pick and shovel instead of running around with a box of blacking and a shoe brush in his hand to shine the shoes of some labor skate grafter, he would be better off and so would we." Another dubbed C.O. Young "Company Young," and labelled him an "avowed enemy of Industrial Unionism." Yet another attacked Young's opposition to immigration and charged that he referred to immigrants as "pauper cast-offs" and "refuse." Young further antagonized Wobblies during the CN and GTP strikes, when he opposed the efforts of B.C. unions to aid the railway workers and belittled them for neglecting "their own suffering members on strike to aid a band of lawless brigands."[12]

But Young need not have worried so much about the support given to the IWW. For while the Vancouver Trades and Labor Council did eventually vote to contribute money and allow its paper to become the official strike bulletin during the struggle, its first impulse was to stifle the unrest. Shortly after the strike broke out, the council sent a delegate into the IWW camps to convince the men to return to work. The effort failed, and as the strike grew, the council reconsidered. It responded to the appeal for help by sending an investigator to check out conditions, and then, some six weeks after the strike began, the VTLC issued a call for aid to its affiliates.[13]

The VTLC, with Socialist Party members at its head, was

quick to use IWW tactics when necessary, but was even quicker to dissociate itself from the Wobblies when their radicalism became inconvenient. During the Vancouver Island miners' strike of 1912-14, the Miners' Liberation League, composed of most of the left-wing parties and unions, adopted many IWW ideas. The League, a defence committee for the striking and imprisoned miners, used children's parades like that pioneered by the IWW in Lawrence, sabotage, and direct action. IWW speakers often appeared on platforms with E. T. Kingsley, Jack Kavanaugh, and J. W. Wilkinson; for a time, a Wobbly headed the League. But when a general strike to free the workers was proposed, the VTLC flatly refused to support it. Though many of the rank and file pushed for such a strike, without the participation of the council and its affiliates the idea was doomed, and it died away.[14]

Not all trade unionists and socialists were opposed to the IWW. Rank and file members of the SPC and the trade unions often had more in common with Wobblies than with their leaders, as events in Nelson, Victoria, and the Miners' Liberation League suggest. But for the most part, the leadership of the unions and the SPC differed bitterly with the ideology and action of the IWW. Though fierce opponents of business unionism, Gomperism, and liberalism, these leaders were equally fierce in their denunciation of the syndicalists. A detailed examination of the Vancouver and Victoria free speech fights shows clearly the different aims of the three organizations, and helps outline some of the reasons behind the charged conflict.

The suppression of radical ideas and organizing has always been an important weapon of the ruling classes. The simplest form of suppression is the outright banning of public meetings, and this has often proved sufficient. In other cases, however, this strategy has prompted a militant response—the free speech fight. The IWW took part in many of these battles, in cities and towns such as Paterson, New Jersey; Victoria, B.C.; San Diego; New Castle, Pennsylvania; and Missoula, Montana.

Most free speech campaigns followed a similar pattern. City officials would object to IWW street meetings, and would pass a by-law prohibiting public speaking. The union would ignore the by-law and step up its efforts. The police would then arrest the soap-box orators and put them in jail to await trial. IWW organizers would put out a call for all available members to travel to the city to carry on the battle. As the cells filled, the city's costs for feeding and guarding the prisoners mounted, until finally civic officials weakened and restored the right to speak in public.

This at least was the IWW theory, but too often civic officials, police, and vigilantes would instead resort to violence to silence the union. Such attacks meant that the IWW paid a high price for its struggle to speak and organize, but the battles were necessary if the union was to continue to spread its message. Furthermore, the Wobblies realized that repression and violence stripped away the state's pretence of being an impartial, neutral arbitrator between capital and labour and revealed it as a tool of the employer.

Like many of the policies and tactics of the IWW, the battles for free speech have been interpreted, debated, and reinterpreted. Joseph Conlin, attempting to fit Wobblies into the American mainstream, has maintained that the fights "were joined to preserve... a right with a Constitutional Article and a century of tradition behind it"; he suggests that the battles were not "hostile or irrelevant to American values." Patrick Renshaw concluded that the fights were waged "not so much to defend a constitutional principle... but to make the world more fully aware of the miserable conditions in which migratory workers lived and labored." Both explanations are much too idealistic. Brissenden presciently countered Conlin's position in 1919, writing that

> The trouble always seems to begin because the local
> authorities are revolted by—or at least nervously
> apprehensive about—either the substance of the IWW
> speeches or the language in which their ideas are conveyed,
> or both. The remarks are alleged to be seditious, incendiary,
> unpatriotic, immoral, etc., or, whether they are any or all
> these or none of them, they are alleged to be profane or
> vulgar beyond the limits of forebearance.[15]

These remarks hardly suggest a sharing of values. Renshaw's contention is also flawed, for the point of the free speech fights was to educate not the world, but the unorganized. Robert Tyler has correctly argued that the fights were "practical defenses of [the] right to organize openly," as well as attempts to recruit and "educate the unorganized and watching workers." Dubofsky has demonstrated that the fights were the only way to organize workers who would soon be shipped to distant camps, where spies and stoolies could quickly spot and eliminate agitators. As one Wobbly wrote, for the migrant workers, "the street corner was their only hall, and if denied the right to agitate there, then they must be silent." Ralph Chaplin, the Wobbly poet who wrote the words to "Solidarity Forever," had this to say about the struggles in a 1960 recollection: "Free speech for what? For a man to get up and try to organize a union. They weren't keeping free speech out—they were keeping unionism out." Henry Frenette wrote that "nearly all the men I have spoken to have heard of the IWW from speakers on the street."[16]

At times, the free speech fights helped bring workers together, as they did in Victoria. But in Vancouver, they drove apart the IWW and the socialist labour leaders. The first significant Vancouver free speech fight occurred in 1909, a prosperous year during which organized labour was increasingly active. The VTLC was busy with plans for a new Labor Temple, and had recently started a monthly paper, the *Western Wage-Earner*. But prices were rising, and events in Vancouver were cause for concern. April saw the end of a bitter longshoreman's strike led by the IWW against the CPR, a strike which was finally broken by the importation of scabs from as far away as Winnipeg. The newly elected city council, headed by an American real estate developer named C.S. Douglas, increasingly took on an anti-labour cant. Mayor Douglas refused to implement the eight-hour day for civic workers, though the measure had been approved in a recent plebiscite. In May, he was to abandon the neutrality of his chairman's role to ensure the passing of a motion to replace city day labourers with contracting out.[17]

The council was also concerned with an influx of migrants from the United States. The increased number of men seeking to enter Vancouver was the result of a clean-up push by the city of Seattle as it prepared for its upcoming Alaska-Yukon-Pacific exposition. On a single April day, Vancouver police prevented nineteen "undesirables" from landing off the Seattle ferry. Migrants who did arrive were tagged with vagrancy or otherwise harassed by police. To justify these actions, the Vancouver police chief maintained that "these men have to be handled firmly right from the start or Vancouver will be overrun with them."[18] This is the context, then, in which the police campaign against free speech took place.

The section of Carrall street between Cordova and Hastings streets had long been established as a place for street speakers. It was the logical place to speak for those who wished to reach a working class audience, for it was in the middle of the workers' community of Vancouver's skid road.[19] A large number of hotels and boarding houses catered to migrants, timber beasts, and the marginally employed. Several unions had offices in the surrounding blocks. The IWW headquarters was at 61 West Cordova, while the SPC was located a few blocks away at 163 West Hastings; in addition, the party maintained a reading room at the Royal Theatre at 124 East Hastings. The Labor Hall, home to several unions as well as the VTLC, was not in the core area, but at 585 Homer, was still close to the action.

On Sunday, 4 April 1909, speakers from both the IWW and the SPC addressed a crowd at the corner of Carrall and Hastings. It was no different from the scores of earlier meetings on the site; even the competition, the Salvation Army, was in its regular place on the opposite corner. This time, however, Vancouver city police ordered the speakers to disperse. When the men refused, they were handed summonses and ordered to appear before the police magistrate two days later.[20] The police contended that the "streets are for people to walk on and people anxious to air their views should hire a hall."[21] The Salvation Army, however, was not asked to disperse. As a writer in the *Western Wage-Earner* remarked pointedly,

> Because workingmen should hold a meeting on a practically deserted thoroughfare and appoint pickets to see that traffic is not impeded, even though a large crowd should gather, will never be accepted as sufficient reason why they should be fined, when at the same time the Salvation Army hold meetings on busy thoroughfares and cause traffic to be blocked, and horses to take fright at the sound of their brass horns and are not molested.[22]

The two sides of the fight were clearly drawn, with the daily press siding with the police. Even the Vancouver *World*, which supported the campaign for the eight-hour day and published the SPC organizer Pettipiece in a weekly "Page for the Wage Earner," took the opportunity to denounce the speakers, arguing that "the blocking of traffic on the streets is a dangerous nuisance," and that the "Socialists" should find "some other space where they could spout to their hearts' content without annoying anyone."[23]

The left swung into action. A well-known socialist attorney,

J.E. Bird, represented the arrested men, and on the day of the trial SPC and IWW members packed the courtroom, only to find that the case was adjourned for a week. To the magistrate's hope that "the offenders would undertake not to repeat the offence in the meantime," Bird retorted that they "would undertake no such thing," and an open air meeting was held on Carrall Street the next evening.[24] The SPC set up a fund for the legal defence and vowed "to take the offensive on the street every evening....Somebody will eventually have to lie down, and we don't know how." The *Industrial Worker* in Spokane noted that "the fight is on," and that "the slaves are preparing for action....There will be a 'hot time in the old town' before long—police or no police!"[25] The VTLC organized a rally at city hall and though the meeting was primarily concerned with the struggle for the eight-hour day, it expressed its "sympathy and pledges its support in maintaining the right of free speech on the streets of Vancouver."[26]

On 13 April the trial of the six men resumed. Again the court was "filled with a strong revolutionary element long before his royal nibs' representative took the bench." But the socialists argued that they had not obstructed the street: they were twelve feet away from the street line, and had put wardens out to maintain order and prevent obstructions. One SPC member, not among the accused, testified on the precautions that had been taken, and even produced a map to show that the thoroughfare had not been obstructed. The defence held that it was clearly discriminatory for a constable to arrest leftists and ignore equally disruptive religionists because they preached a creed more acceptable to the police.

This legalistic defence was juxtaposed with a spirit of resistance among the Wobblies. William Taylor, exemplifying the kind of erudition of many IWW members, took objection to swearing on the Bible, complaining that it could harbour germs. He argued that he had not been ordered to disperse, but only to stop speaking. Armed with a dictionary, he contended that the verb "to disperse" meant "to cause to break up or to scatter." This being the case, it was obviously grammatically and anatomically impossible for him to accede to the alleged police demand that he disperse himself![27] The case was again adjourned, this time until the following Wednesday. The defense attorney hinted that his clients would take jail sentences rather than pay fines, and warned that "the game would be kept up until the jail was packed."[28]

The battle on the street continued. On 19 April, the magistrate finally rendered judgement. Taylor was found guilty and ordered to pay either a fine of $5 and costs of $2.50—about three days' pay for an unskilled worker—or serve ten days in jail with hard labour, double the usual sentence for being drunk and disorderly. The magistrate advised that if Taylor's conviction did not put an end to the meetings, "the punishment will be much more heavier next time." The crown withdrew the charges against the other defendants.[29]

But the magistrate's leniency went unappreciated. The Vancouver *Province*, using a cavalier rendering of the IWW's name, reported on 2 May that

> A mass meeting was held last night in the front of City Hall under the auspices of the United Workmen of the World. There was a fair attendance, and Mr. J. Jenkins [Arthur Jenkins of Vancouver local 322] was in the chair. There were several speakers, who advocated most strongly the principles and ideas of the revolutionists.[30]

The failure of Bird's subsequent appeal had little effect on the militants. Indeed, it hardly came as a surprise to the IWW. The secretary of local 322 wrote before the B.C. Supreme Court judgement that

> It matters not to us which way the decision is handed down: whether for or against us, we shall still uphold our constitutional right of free speech and the right to peaceably assemble for the purpose of discussing our views on this great social problem.[31]

On 13 May, "local Anarchists and Socialists" gathered to listen to Lucy Parsons, widow of Haymarket martyr Albert Parsons and a founder of the IWW. The daily newspapers were unimpressed with her "recitation [of] the unjust murder of her husband," but Parsons's visit provided a rallying point for the Vancouver activists. William Taylor addressed the crowd despite the warnings of the police magistrate, and demanded the restoration of free speech. Two days later, the SPC called for another mass meeting at the city hall, and noted that the fiery Comrade James Hawthornthwaite, Socialist MLA from Nanaimo, had been invited to come and take part in the fray. The *Western Clarion* also reminded readers that it was the duty of those who did not go to jail to help raise money for those who did.[32]

That same day, police arrested T.M. Beamish, a Socialist real estate broker, and charged him with obstructing the thoroughfare. Beamish, copying Taylor's courtroom tactics, argued that he had climbed up on a water trough to address the crowd. This meant that the order to disperse himself implied that he should drop to the ground and splatter on the pavement. This he was reluctant to do, and he suggested that a call for suicide exceeded the constable's authority. Unpersuaded, the police magistrate sentenced Beamish to pay a fine of $100 or serve thirty days with hard labour.[33]

To protest the outrageous fine, the SPC organized a meeting at the city hall for 17 May. The large crowd was addressed by Beamish; J.H. McVety, a machinist who was president of the VTLC, manager of the *Western Wage-Earner*, and a member of the SPC; E.T. Kingsley, the proprietor of a print shop and a prominent socialist; and L.T. English, a printer who belonged to the International Typographical Union and the SPC.[34] The following night, upwards of one thousand people gathered on the traditional battlefield of Carrall and Hastings. The speaker refused to give his name to the police, and at this point, a sergeant and four constables "moved off like the whipped curs they always are when they run up against a person who has the manhood or womanhood to stand true to their own convictions," as the *Industrial Worker* put it. The *Western Clarion* contented itself with noting that the five "waddled solemnly up the street like a flock of fat ducks."[35]

The following day one case brought before the court was dismissed, while later that night, the IWW-led meeting at Hastings and Carrall was observed but not disrupted by the police. They attempted to take the name of one speaker, but when he refused to give it, the police simply moved on.[36]

This signalled the end of overt police harassment. The Crown did not press the arrests to the full extent of the law, the police backed down quickly, and the progressive forces could claim a clear-cut victory.[37] It even appeared that solidarity in the face of a common enemy was possible, that the labour movement, the SPC, and the IWW could forget their ideological differences and work together. But the solidarity was more imagined than real.

The socialists, trade unionists, and Wobblies differed greatly on ends and means, and the three groups reacted in conflicting ways. In examining these tactical differences, we learn more about each group and the strands that made up the B.C. labour and left movements.

The reaction of the Vancouver Trades and Labour Council was by far the most restrained. The minutes of its bi-weekly meetings reveal that the free speech issue was far down on the council's list of priorities. The public meeting held by the trade unionists on 10 April was primarily aimed not at securing free speech, but rather the eight-hour day for civic workers. Much was made of the Laurier government's proposed naval bill, and the pages of the minutes are filled with stirring speeches, many made by the council secretary, Parm Pettipiece. The upcoming May Day celebrations were of vital concern, but even these were overshadowed by another event. Nearly a third of one meeting that took place during the free speech campaign was devoted to a discussion of a football that had been lost by or stolen from a visiting union team. Free speech was mentioned only once in the VTLC minutes: as noted above, the issue was tacked on to a resolution condemning the actions of Magistrate Williams. This resolution took place on 20 May—one week after the arrests had stopped and the battle won save for the withdrawal of the charge against English.

The monthly paper of the VTLC, the *Western Wage-Earner*, likewise paid little attention to the events on the city streets. The April issue made no mention of the fight, while an article in May gave only the sketchiest of details. It contained no hard facts and gave no names of those arrested; it mentioned neither the SPC nor the IWW. Instead of a call for action or a plea for funds, the May issue weakly expressed the "hope that the case will be fought to the last ditch." It made no suggestion as to who should fight to the last ditch or how labour should contribute.[38]

An article in the June edition of the *Western Wage-Earner* tied the campaign for free speech to the dismissal of the unpopular police magistrate Williams, just as the VTLC resolution of 20 May had. The magistrate certainly did need a reprimand: men who had slept in a CPR box car were sentenced to six months with double leg irons, while a strike breaker who assaulted a seventy-year-old man with a hammer received only thirty days. But it is clear that the VTLC saw the free speech agitation largely as another way to discredit the official. The *Western Wage-Earner* was unequivocal:

> The feeling against the police magistrate has at last taken definite form, thanks to the men who use the streets [as] a forum, and probably had such unjust punishment not been inflicted on street speakers the juvenile offenders might have been subject to the caprice of Mr. Williams for years to come. The mass meeting in the city hall decided in no uncertain manner the course necessary to remedy matters.[39]

The "necessary" course adopted, however, was hardly earth-shattering—the council voted to circulate a copy of the meeting's resolution to other unions as well as city officials.

A study of the minutes of the Vancouver city council reveals another interesting facet. During the free speech fight, the VTLC sent two communications to city council, one which was presented at the meeting of 10 May, the other at the meeting of 25 May. The first was "re 8 hour day and entertainment of Japanese squadron," the latter point stemming from city outlays to wine and dine officers of visiting Japanese naval ships. The second letter concerned the establishment of a juvenile court, and was part of the agitation against Magistrate Williams. Neither communication mentioned the free speech fight.[40]

The VTLC was only marginally interested in the free speech issue. The trade union movement had already established its political program, and stuck doggedly to it during the battle; it continued to prefer footballs to soapboxes. Some members, especially those connected to the SPC, did address public meetings, but the council as a body did little to confront the city officials or support the men who did. Instead, the VTLC preferred to privately petition the mayor. The council meeting of 3 June heard a report from James McVety in which he stated that the joint VTLC/SPC committee had met with Mayor Douglas and had alleged that the police were discriminating against the workers. The committee had made it known that "no objection would be taken if everyone was prevented from speaking," but that strong objections would continue until equal privileges were given to all.[41]

The wording of this report is revealing. It outlines a unity between the trade union movement and the SPC that is not apparent from a reading of the newspapers, including the *Wage-*

Earner and the *Western Clarion*. It further suggests that the VTLC/ SPC committee was prepared to accept a total ban on public speaking, that it sought only equitable treatment before the law. This was a much more moderate position than the demand for free speech. It also implies an acceptance of the right of the state to ban public speaking, an argument that the IWW and other elements of the SPC were not willing to grant. The joint committee's threat to the mayor is likewise illuminating. The promise to continue "strong objections" in the face of police harassment pales beside the *Western Clarion*'s vow to fight in the streets and the IWW's call to fill the jail with agitators. The threat implies a reluctance on the part of the trade union bureaucrats and the professional politicians of the SPC to maintain a campaign of direct action. The haste with which the free speech issue was tied to the council's own program of the eight-hour day and judicial reform further suggests that on this occasion the most influential labour leaders were happy to use the IWW agitation for their own ends. It is noteworthy that McVety claimed that the VTLC's quiet diplomacy with the mayor was more important than the IWW's resistance in the streets and courtroom theatrics. He reported that the VTLC/SPC joint committe had conferred with Mayor Douglas, who had "taken action and no further trouble had resulted."[42]

A further notice in the *Western Wage-Earner* is equally inflated. In the July issue, the paper reported that the

> prompt action on the part of the Trades and Labor Council and the Socialist Party saved a lot of trouble over the question of street speaking. The two bodies appointed a committee who waited upon the chairman of the Police Commission and alleged that the police were discriminating against the workers and in favour of the Salvation Army. The matter has been investigated and police have apparently been instructed not to allow their personal feelings to influence them in the matter.[43]

From the experience of the Vancouver free speech fight and the scores of free speech fights waged across North America, it is unreasonable to assume that these labour statesmen had the power attributed to them by the *Wage-Earner*. It is more likely that the police were acting on their own initiative rather than on orders from the city council, probably as part of the campaign against

American migrants. But the rank and file of the Socialist Party and the IWW were able to mount a rapid counter-attack against the police; both groups quickly organized defence committees and staged large open-air meetings. In this respect they were far superior to the trade unionists. In the face of this spontaneous reaction, the police, without the explicit backing of the council and the courts, were reluctant to proceed.[44]

The role of the SPC in the free speech fight is more confused and contradictory. Despite the party's propaganda against trade unionism, leaders were quick to join with their trade council counterparts and were willing to seek the same compromises as the VTLC. There is also a suggestion that the leadership of the SPC was more than willing to cut a deal with the city fathers in order to allow both sides to retreat gracefully. The Vancouver *World* reported on 28 May that a charge against Socialist Party member Leo English was withdrawn because "the Socialists have agreed to conduct their meetings in the future so that the street will not be blocked." The *Western Clarion* denied this charge a week later, but the denial is interesting:

> . . . the police Prosecutor stated he would withdraw the case as the Socialists had agreed to so conduct their meetings as not to block the traffic. As the Socialists had agreed to do nothing of the kind, though they do make a practice of conducting their meetings with a little decency, it may be presumed that this is a graceful way for the police to climb down.[45]

It is hard to know just what to make of this argument. But the willingness of the SPC to join with trade union leadership in order to seek a compromise with city officials, even after the fight had been won in the streets, suggests that the leadership of the SPC was uneasy with the rough and tumble approach taken by the IWW.

The free speech fight of 1909 brought out a range of responses from the left-wing and labour organizations of the city. The migrant, disenfranchised members of the IWW had little recourse other than direct action, and they were prepared to face imprisonment. The skilled workers of the trade unions had less reason to oppose vigourously the harassment of police, and they preferred to avoid jail and fight back with entreaties and letters of protest.

Socialists were torn between those such as Pettipiece, who sided with the labour organization, and others who were prepared to back up radical rhetoric with militancy in the streets.

Such antagonism does not appear to have existed in Victoria during its free speech fight in 1911. City officials told unionists, Wobblies, and socialists that they could no longer speak on any street corner: their meetings were to be restricted to a site far from the downtown traffic. The Salvation Army and other religious groups, however, were not banned from the city centre. On 21 July, the IWW started soapboxing in earnest to protest the prohibition. Police stopped and arrested four Wobblies and one SPC member, charging them with vagrancy. On the next day, the two organizations held a joint meeting at the corner of Government and Yates streets. Fifteen were arrested. Tellingly, the meeting took place on the same spot as a Salvation Army meeting, and began just after the religious order had finished up. A sympathetic crowd of about two thousand jostled the police and refused to leave, all the while hurling a tirade of abuse at police. Later, the IWW organizer J.S. Biscay arrived and tried to reason with the prosecuting attorney, the chief of police, and the mayor. When warned that anyone who violated the by-law would be deported, Biscay retorted that deportation would be welcomed by the migrant workers, for it would mean a free ticket home. Biscay also pointed out that other cities had tried to stop the IWW from speaking and had failed. Failure was especially likely in Victoria, he added, because the IWW and the SPC were completely united on the issue. The Victoria Trades and Labor Council issued a powerful condemnation of the attempt to silence the speakers, calling it "part of a plan to defeat the workers in bettering their condition." The council warned that class war was inevitable and on the horizon, and in the meantime, labour demanded equal treatment with the religious groups. In the face of this united opposition, city council retreated. Though complete free speech was not restored, the labour speakers were accorded treatment equal to that of the Salvation Army. Seven Wobblies were sentenced to a fine of $20 or ten days in jail, and each chose to serve the time so that the money "will remain in the pockets of the workers and the city will feed the workers." The IWW dared the city to "show us just where they have won anything in this free speech fight. . . . We have freedom of speech, the food and lodging, and the fines stowed away in our jeans. What did you get out of it, Mr. Boss?"[46]

The events of the 1912 Vancouver free speech fight show that solidarity was not always extended as it had been in Victoria. The context of this next and better-known round of the struggle was markedly different. The winter of 1911-12 signalled the beginning of the end of the pre-war boom. Unemployment reached critical levels as laid-off workers from railway construction and logging camps made their way to Vancouver. Meanwhile the Salvation Army, government officials, and civic "boosters" encouraged migrant workers to head to the province to ensure a cheap labour supply for the planned spring railway construction. One contractor observed that "in all my experience in railway construction, I never saw the supply of labor so ample as it is this winter. For several weeks I have been turning down over 100 applicants daily."[47] The city was responsible for the existing primitive forms of welfare, but it did little to alleviate the situation. The civic labour bureau was swamped with more than five hundred applicants, but could find only temporary, part-time work for fewer than a hundred. The IWW held street meetings to organize the unemployed, and several protest meetings were held. The response of the city was to crack down on vagrants and transients. Twenty-three men were "vagged" on a single day, and the chief of police complained that "the city is at present over-run with undesirables."[48] But the street protests increased, and alarmed citizens elected James Findlay, a law-and-order candidate and former head of the Vancouver Conservative machine, to the mayor's office.

Findlay was regarded as a pro-business candidate, and he did not disappoint his backers. He called for an "iron hand" to deal with the unrest on the streets, and city council passed a by-law forbidding all outdoor meetings. On 20 January, the Saturday following the passage of the by-law, the IWW held a meeting at the corner of Cordova and Carrall. At this meeting, four men were arrested; three were charged with vagrancy and one with assaulting a police officer. The following day, six were arrested during a meeting on Powell and Carrall.[49]

The arrests galvanized the unionists and leftists of Vancouver. The IWW and the SPC called another meeting for the following

Sunday. The VTLC decided to support the move to prove that "freedom of speech in the British Empire is guaranteed by higher authority than any city administration."[50] On 28 January, a crowd of several thousand gathered to hear R.P. Pettipiece report on his meeting with the provincial government on the issue of unemployment. The deputy chief of police declared the meeting illegal, and arrested Pettipiece. When protests were made, the deputy chief signalled to a waiting line of mounted and foot patrolmen who waded into the crowd, swinging clubs and horsewhips. The *Province* reporter noted that "those not fortunate enough to get out of the way went down like ten-pins before the irresistible onslaught of the officers. . . . The Powell Street Grounds looked something like a battlefield."[51] Nearly thirty people were arrested, and bail was set at five hundred dollars apiece. While James McVety and J.W. Wilkinson, president of the VTLC, bailed out Pettipiece, the outrageous bond kept many others in jail—fourteen were still imprisoned three days later.[52] Authorities moved to seal the border to keep Wobblies from flooding the city, and even the inter-urban B.C. Electric Railway was carefully watched to prevent the feared invasion.[53]

Subsequent meetings were broken up by the police. Arrests for vagrancy increased markedly as authorities used the vague wording of the criminal code to harass the workers. In one attempt to evade police, Wobblies and SPC members rented boats off Stanley Park and spoke to the crowds through a huge megaphone. But the strong currents and police worked together to break up the armada: the megaphone was scuttled and the protestors were arrested when they finally docked.[54]

As with the 1909 episode, the free speech fight of 1912 can be interpreted as a victory for the left/labour movement, as an example of the need for and desire of the organizations to forget sectarian politics to face a common enemy. Indeed, at the 1 February meeting of the VTLC, Pettipiece himself told delegates that "it was up to them to associate themselves with the IWW, as a large number of the members of this organization were coming to the city for the purpose of compelling the authorities to show their hand."[57] Later in the meeting, a committee was named to "co-operate with [the] committee from [the] Socialist Party and the IWW in [the] fight for free speech and work for the unemployed."[58]

But the willingness of the VTLC/SPC alliance to separate itself from the IWW was evident from the start. The two organizations had done little to organize the first protests among the unemployed, preferring to petition the local and provincial governments. These governments were quite prepared to ignore the requests of the respectable groups, as Pettipiece himself acknowledged during his speech of 28 January, but neither the trades union movement nor the leaders of the SPC were prepared to organize the unorganized in the manner of the IWW.[59]

Only four days after Pettipiece's call for unity, the *B.C. Federationist* cautiously sought to deny the importance of street meetings:

> The edict goes forth that no more street meetings are to be held. As this has evidently applied to all organizations which have been in the habit of using the streets for such purposes, there is no reasonable ground for complaint. Street meetings, of whatever character, have always been a nuisance, and it is more than doubtful that enough good ever accrued to any cause through such meetings.... If the edict clearing the streets is made permanent and enforced against all alike, there should be no complaint from anyone.

Further in the editorial, the paper began to separate the respectable, resident labour leaders from the IWW members who had begun the fight:

> The speakers who were to address the gathering [of 28 January] mostly belonged to Vancouver, some of them being officials of the Vancouver Trades and Labor Council, and among the most widely known men in the labor movement in Canada. In spite of all this, however, it was ordained by the government that this gathering must not be allowed.[60]

The editorial makes clear the trade union contention that the issue was equal treatment before the law, not the right to organize. By emphasizing that the speakers of 28 January were local union officials rather than foreign agitators, the article hints that a campaign against the IWW should not be strongly protested, but that the harassment of respectable leaders would not go unnoticed. This stands in stark contrast to the *Industrial Worker's* editorial of 1 February, which heralds the apparent solidarity among the union and socialist movement:

The Trades and Labor Assembly [sic] has gone on record as being in favor of free speech and assemblage and as being willing to back up that right. The SP of C are also backing the men, and this co-operation of forces regardless of differences, means that Vancouver will be in receipt of the dose that made other cities sit up and take notice.[61]

The IWW called for men and money to come to Vancouver to join the battle. It hinted at rumours of a general strike, and opined that "that such a strike would be accompanied with the workers' weapon—SABOTAGE—there is but little doubt."[62] J.S. Biscay, an organizer for the union who would play a large role in the Canadian Northern strike later in the year, declared at meetings and in the press that "if they want to down free speech in Vancouver they will have to bury us with it." Another Wobbly declared that "we will have free speech in Vancouver or else make the grass grow in the streets." The IWW's response to the repression was direct action and confrontation through intensifying the pressure on the civic authorities, typified by its threat to have members "keep travelling to Vancouver until the city gets enough and is willing to say so."[63]

The response of the SPC was varied, as it had been in 1909. Some members, such as William Watts, made it clear that "when the real fighting takes place, there you will find us striking out, shoulder to shoulder for a common cause." Another writer drew parallels with the Russian nihilists and proclaimed that "every Cossack's whip that makes a mark on any part of my anatomy will be avenged by me if life is left in my body to avenge it."[64]

But another writer decried violence, and in an editorial entitled "Get the Power," remarked, "What can you do? Just one thing: Be the State." On 11 February, Hawthornthwaite moved to take the battle off the streets by announcing that the SPC and VTLC would send a deputation to the mayor. In doing so, he argued, the SPC

was following along the lines of reasonable political action. They would ask for the right which was being denied them of meeting, not on the crowded thoroughfares of the city, but in some square or park. If those rights were refused, they would consider what other steps to take. As far as the Socialist Party of Canada was concerned, it would do its level best to win that right.

At the same meeting, Wilfred Gribble, a writer and organizer for the SPC, advised the audience "to become interested in the question of organization . . . and to send members of their own class to parliament."[65]

Thus the leaders of the SPC and the VTLC agreed that direct action was not appropriate. They further agreed to forego the right to speak on the streets, unlike the IWW, in favour of the right to speak only on designated sites. The Trades and Labor Council resolution passed at its 1 February meeting was strong in its condemnation of the police riots, but weak in its call for action: the meeting resolved that council delegates were to bring the matter before their unions and ask that the unions help by purchasing picture postcards of the police charge. It further resolved that the council ask the provincial government to select a commission to investigate the administration of the city police.[66]

By channelling the protests away from the streets and into government chambers, the trade unions leaders and SPC sought to restore peace quickly and deprive the IWW of its leadership role. It is clear from the historical record that solidarity was extended to the IWW only when it controlled the street action and had to be included. When the time came to hammer out a peace accord, the leadership of the two groups used the threats of anarchism and an IWW "invasion" as a club. To make the strategy work, the SPC and VTLC sought to replace the IWW as the leader in the free speech campaign. It could best do this by shifting the battleground. When they had taken control of the fight, the two groups could then jettison the IWW and make a deal.

Labour leaders and socialist politicians moved to change the venue of the free speech battle. On the weekend of 10-11 February, both Pettipiece and Hawthornthwaite cancelled scheduled appearances at the street meetings. They preferred instead to work on plans for the meeting with the mayor. When questioned about his absence, Pettipiece replied, "it isn't good warfare to put the generals in the front of the battle."[67]

On the morning of 12 February, the long-anticipated meeting with the mayor and police commissioners took place. The representatives of the VTLC and SPC were Hawthornthwaite, Wilkinson, J. McMillan, a vice-president of the VTLC, James McVety, and Victor Midgley. No rank and file members were included, and the IWW was explicitly excluded from the meeting by the delegation. Two Wobblies representing the union went to the city hall at the time of the meeting and demanded to be included in the conference. Stopped by city council aides, the men sent a note to the delegation. Wilkinson came out and attempted to pacify the men by telling them that "I told them [the police commissioners] that the trades and labor people wanted to interview them, and so they do not want to have you in just now." He promised to try to have the commissioners meet with them later, and returned to the meeting. But it quickly became apparent that the VTLC and SPC leaders in fact wanted to cut out the IWW from the rest of the movement. When the commissioners were questioned by the press on the steps of the city hall after the meeting, the mayor outlined the arguments presented by the delegation. He reiterated the city's determination to "rid the city of the 'lawless element,'" and bluntly stated that "the unions had nothing in common with the men who were waging the fight for free speech." The VTLC and SPC decision to eliminate the IWW was made even clearer by one of the commissioners. Asked if they would meet with the IWW, the commissioner replied that

> The Trades and Labor delegation repudiated the two Industrial Workers so that was why they were not permitted to join the conference. When the Workers tried to get in the labor men said they were not on the delegation, and had no rightful part in the morning's session. Therefore we told them that we could not see them.[68]

A story in the Vancouver *Sun* the following day suggests that the commissioner's account was correct, and that the exclusion of the IWW was at least as much the idea of the delegation as of the civic authorities. The report noted that in contrast to the rough stance of the IWW, the delegates had "pointed out that if tact and sagacity were used there would be no disturbance of the peace on the part of the labor or socialist party."[69] Finally, a curious statement made by Victor Midgley hints at the plan to separate the Trades and Labor Council and the Socialist Party from the IWW. Denying that the delegation had repudiated the Wobblies, Midgley asserted that "the real reason the IWW was not admitted was because they [sic] did not figure on the committee."[70] This Jesuitical logic is further proof that the delegation wanted to discredit the IWW and make a separate peace.

The delegates were prepared to be eminently reasonable and to seek a compromise. Wilkinson stated later that the meeting had been called "in order that the labor men might present a formal application for free speech rights on public squares." The *Province* noted that Wilkinson "carefully pointed out 'public squares,' not 'public streets.'"[71] Despite the unassuming request of the delegation, the authorities were not prepared to compromise. The commission expressed a desire to allow free speech on the Powell street grounds "just as soon as conditions in this city became normal again," but would not give assurances that the meetings planned for 18 February would be unmolested. This could not be accepted even by the less militant representatives, and they prepared to go to Victoria.[72] They planned to use the threat of a rabid IWW as the main bargaining chip to effect a compromise. In a statement to the press, the delegates indicated that

> If the dictates of the labor body are carried out the
> momentous question will be fought to the last ditch by all
> the legal machinery available, and not by the more drastic
> measures urged by other organizations outside the labor
> party.... [Pettipiece] contended that the truth of the matter
> was Canada had been made the dumping ground of the
> world.[73]

On 17 February, Wilkinson and McVety met with McBride and his cabinet. They argued that the repression had only strengthened the IWW, that,

> granting that the IWW men were all that their most
> persistent maligners made them out to be, the proclamation
> prohibiting open-air meetings was most ill-advised and
> inexpedient since it had simply been recognized by trouble-
> makers the continent over as an invitation to come to
> Vancouver. The man in the street, they averred, had
> scarcely heard of the IWW until Mayor Findlay entered into
> a conflict with the people who wanted to hold open-air
> meetings.[74]

Thus the delegation, the mayor, and the premier were agreed that the IWW must go; the difference was really only over tactics. The subtleties of the social democrats and senior government were more effective than the ham-handed reaction of the municipal Tories, if they were less satisfactory viscerally.

On 18 February, another mass meeting was held in the streets.

This time, however, it was peaceful. A police commissioner explained that the "objection heretofore at Powell street had been the use of seditious and obscene language. This was absent yesterday and accordingly the police did not interfere." This was obviously untrue, and was nothing more than a transparent attempt to save face. The newspapers revealed a more convincing explanation. The premier, about to introduce controversial bills in the legislature, had his own reason for forcing a settlement. The bills called for the creation of the Pacific Great Eastern railway, and the loans for construction, guaranteed by the province, would have to be raised on foreign markets. The latest provincial budget called for a deficit of six million dollars, while the city of Vancouver was preparing to issue three million dollars' worth of stocks: all of this money would have to be supplied by international lenders. British papers were already carrying reports of four thousand rioters in the streets of British Columbia and men killed in the tumult, and this publicity hardly presented a picture of stability and peace for investors. Furthermore, a provincial election had just been called, and though the Conservative government had no fear of losing the election, riots and police brutality would not help the Tories.[75]

If Premier McBride wanted a quick, peaceful end to the free speech fights, so too did the socialists and trade unionists. Both groups had high hopes for the election, and their tactics during the free speech campaign were geared to aid the political struggle. The socialists and their trade union allies needed to whip up emotions to strengthen their support, but needed to channel those emotions away from the streets and towards the ballot box. Throughout the free speech battle, the VTLC and SPC plumped for political action and organization. At the meeting of 18 February, socialist speakers urged the crowd to "go to the ballot, that is the remedy. Get on the voters' list." The attempt to take over the free speech fight appeared to work. The Vancouver *Sun* noted that the 18 February meeting "served to demonstrate that the battle for the privilege of street speaking is not led solely by the Industrial Workers of the World." The following day, the *Sun* outlined the reasons Hawthornthwaite had for seeking a political resolution to the struggle:

> ...the alliance formed between Mr. Hawthornthwaite and Premier McBride some years ago, when the government of

which Mr. McBride is the head was compelled to depend
upon Socialistic support for its existence, has never been
entirely dissolved....An election is to take place very soon
and Mr. McBride and Mr. Hawthornthwaite both wish to
capture all the votes they can. Mr. Hawthornthwaite will of
course, be a candidate for Nanaimo and his election will
depend upon the Socialists of that constituency....Mr.
Hawthornthwaite will receive from the Socialists of Nanaimo
credit for his attack upon the Vancouver police and he will
have it spread...that it was owing to his intervention that
free-speech of the soap-box variety is allowed here.[76]

Committed to electoral politics, the SPC and VTLC sought a
compromise, and needed one, as proof of the effectiveness of their
strategy. In order to shift the fight to the provincial election, and
afterwards perhaps to treat with the Conservatives, the two
groups had to disown the IWW and discredit its strategy of direct
action. The *B.C. Federationist* set out the socialist line clearly:

Provincial general elections set for early date in April. What
can we do about it? There is only one thing we can do just
now. Educate and organize the working class to the end that
they may seize the powers of the State and get behind the
guns instead of in front of them. To meet the violence of the
police with violence would be the most foolish and suicidal
policy possible.[77]

No doubt meeting violence with violence would have been
suicidal. But no one, save a lone writer in the *Western Clarion*, had
advocated violence. Equating the direct action tactic of flooding
the jails with the use of violence was simply another way of repu-
diating the IWW. The VTLC/SPC argument was clear—direct
action and violence were interchangeable; violence was a doomed
tactic; therefore direct action was doomed.

On 21 February, after his own trip to Victoria, Mayor Findlay
met with the free speech delegation. This time, IWW leaders were
included and presented with a *fait accompli*. The terms of the peace
treaty were outlined. No meetings were to be held on public
streets, but public squares were free for open-air meetings. The
mayor would move to quash the indictments against the arrested
men, and the prisoners would be released. In return, the
defendants were to promise not to take legal proceedings against
the city. But the city authorities reneged even on this watered-

down resolution. While free speech was allowed, the charges were not dropped and the prisoners were not released. Only the IWW protested the betrayal, vowing to continue the fight until the promises had been met.[78] While there is some evidence that they did protest, the local became involved in conflicts it acknowledged to be more important—the Lawrence strike and the San Diego free speech fight.

A later incident gives some insight into the differences between the IWW and the SPC and VTLC, and suggests the lengths to which the socialist and labour leaders would go to separate themselves from the revolutionaries. On 1 March, five of the men arrested on 28 January, who decided to take a quick trial by judge rather than wait until May for a trial by jury, were sentenced. Another, John Taylor, had his case dismissed. Taylor and William Love denied that they belonged to the IWW; the other four admitted that they were Wobblies. Love was sentenced to three months from the date of his arrest, while the IWW members were given three months from the date of sentencing. Part of the evidence used against the men was a telegram sent on 12-13 February by Vincent St. John, the IWW general-secretary, to Mayor Findlay. The telegram, widely regarded as an inflammatory intervention by a foreigner, stated,

> The entire organization supports Vancouver Workers in their efforts to maintain free speech. The rights of the members of this organization will be enforced in spite of all the corporation lice holding political jobs in the Dominion of Canada. Free speech will be established and maintained in Vancouver, if it takes twenty years. Hold you personally responsible for any injury inflicted upon members of this organization by Cossacks under your control.[79]

Both McVety and Pettipiece were called to testify at the trial. Presumably called by the defence, their testimony was carefully weighted to remove the "respectable" leaders from the "rough" members of the IWW. McVety stated that

> I believe in free speech, but I do not believe that force will avail against the constituted authorities. I believe that free speech is now established in this province. It is still further my belief that Vincent St. John's telegram sent to the mayor from Chicago will have a bad effect upon the membership of the IWW in Canada.

This statement implies that the IWW had in fact advocated violence, and it could not have helped the men on trial. Pettipiece
was even more forceful. In spite of his early appeal for solidarity,
he claimed at the trial that "the organization known as the IWW
is a product of existing social conditions. I do not approve of
them, and I am most certainly opposed to the St. John telegram."
Asked if he approved of the IWW's existence, he replied, "No; but
they are like the trusts and other big aggregations. I don't approve
of those, but I have to take them." His dislike of large labour
unions faded away quickly, for a few months later, Pettipiece
addressed the VTLC and announced that "workers must get wise
to the fact that what was needed is bigger unions and less unions."
Clearly, it was the IWW, not some abstract notion of monopoly,
that he detested.[80]

An examination of the arrested men shows that it was in fact
the IWW and the rank and file of the SPC who mounted the campaign for free speech and were the main targets of repression. The
names of 42 men arrested for violations of the street by-law, unlawful assembly, obstruction of police officers, or vagrancy in
connection with the fight for free speech can be gleaned from the
newspapers of the day. Of this number, eleven cannot be identified with any political organization. It is likely, however, that
most of them belonged to or were sympathetic to the IWW. Newspaper accounts state that the men arrested on 28 January were
Wobblies or SPC members, and the *Western Clarion* identified only
eight of the men as Socialist Party members. This strongly suggests that the other men, including many of those who cannot be
placed in a particular political group, were in fact connected to
the IWW.

Seventeen of the men can be positively identified as IWW
members. Two others denied that they were Wobblies at their
trials. Nine are identified as SPC members, while two others are
named as "Socialists." Only two trade union officials were among
the arrested men: Parm Pettipiece and George Nicholl, identified
as a delegate to the Laborers' Union and an officer of the Civic
Employees' Union. It is possible that this is the same George
Nicholl arrested in 1909, as the IWW had worked to organize
both labourers and civic workers; furthermore, Nicholl called
William Coombs, an IWW cook, to give testimony at his trial.[81]

This cataloguing of the arrested men suggests that while

VTLC and SPC leaders were prepared to give fiery speeches and serve on delegations, they were not prepared to face arrest and jail. Pettipiece himself gives strength to this argument through his actions at the earlier trial of the IWW men, and his statement at his own trial on 19 May 1912. Despite the fact that the *Western Clarion* and the *B.C. Federationist*, which he edited, had claimed that the 28 January meeting had been called primarily to test the free-speech ban, Pettipiece announced that when he attended the meeting, "I did not know anything about it being a free speech fight."[82]

The leaders of the labour movement and the SPC chose to occupy a very different position in the struggle than the militants of the SPC and the IWW. Opposed to direct action, they placed their faith in the upcoming election, hoping for the return of a healthy Socialist slate by workers who had heeded their admonition that "the weapon wherein lies your salvation is your pen... use this peaceful weapon at the ballot box."[83] The Conservatives, to no one's surprise, swept into power on 28 March; the Liberals were eliminated from the provincial parliament, but the Socialists returned only two deputies. Most of the eighteen SPC candidates did not poll enough voters to reclaim their deposits.[84] In deciding to abandon a common front in favour of parliamentary politics, the trade unions and the SPC ensured that the IWW would be weakened and that rank and file militancy would be hampered. In return, the labour and socialist leaders proved unable to achieve anything on their chosen battleground. Chances for a real solidarity and organization of the unemployed were squandered on the chimera of social democracy.

Notes for Chapter 3

1. *Western Clarion*, 15 July, 22 July 1905.
2. *Western Clarion*, 6 July, 31 August 1912.
3. *Western Clarion*, 6 July, 8 June 1912.
4. *Western Wage-Earner*, February 1910.
5. *Western Wage-Earner*, July 1909.
6. *Western Wage-Earner*, February 1910.
7. *Western Wage-Earner*, April 1910
8. *Western Wage-Earner*, October 1910.
9. *IUB*, 17 August 1907.

10. *B.C. Federationist*, 16 January 1914; McCormack, p. 113; William Z. Foster, *Pages from a Worker's Life*. New York: International Publishers, 1970, p. 138; Foner, *The IWW*, pp. 427-428; *Solidarity*, 18 April 1914.

11. McCormack, p. 111; Robert H. Babcock, *Gompers in Canada: A Study in American Continentalism before the First World War*. Toronto: University of Toronto Press, 1974, pp. 137-142. Morrison is cited on p. 137; *IW*, 29 May 1913.

12. Carlos Schwantes, *Radical Heritage: Labor, Socialism, and Reform in Washington and British Columbia, 1885-1917*. Vancouver: Douglas and McIntyre, 1979, p. 138; Foner, *The IWW*, p. 184; *IW*, 11 June 1910, 16 March 1911, 19 June 1913; Foner, *The IWW*, p. 231.

13. *IW*, 11 April 1912; *B.C. Federationist*, 22 June 1912; Phillips, p. 53.

14. *B.C. Federationist*, 7 November, 14 November, 5 December 1913; *Sun*, 9 December 1913; *B.C. Federationist*, 16 January 1914; Phillips, p. 60.

15. Conlin, p. 74; Patrick Renshaw, *The Wobblies: The Story of Syndicalism in the United States*. New York: Anchor Books, 1968, p. 84; Brissenden, p. 263.

16. Robert L. Tyler, *Rebels of the Woods: The IWW in the Pacific Northwest*. Eugene: University of Oregon Books, 1967, p. 33; Dubofsky, pp. 174-175; cited in Foner, *"Fellow Workers and Friends,"* p. 12; Joe Glazier, *Songs for Woodworkers*. Portland, Oregon: Collector Records, 1977; Frenette cited in McCormack, pp. 105-106.

17. Phillips, *No Power Greater*, p. 55, implies that the three organizations—the IWW, the VTLC, and the SPC—worked together to defeat the ban on speaking. McCormack does give the IWW the leading role in the battle, but makes no mention of the deep divisions among the groups. Foner, *The IWW*, likewise assumes a high degree of unity. Scott does point out the splits in the labour movement, but attributes them to "craft internationals" and ignores deeper political motives, pp. 41-51. See Phillips, *No Power Greater*, p. 49, for general conditions. For the longshoremen's strike, see *Province*, 5 April 1909; for the eight-hour day and Mayor Douglas's role, see *World*, 17 April 1909; *Western Wage-Earner,*, April and May 1909. For contracting out, see *World*, 11 May 1909; *Province*, 11 May 1909. Strictly speaking, the 1909 battle was not the first in Vancouver. In 1907, the VTLC and SPC formed a Free Speech League to combat harassment and arrests. Little came of it; as Phillips notes, "Before a serious situation could develop, a new wave of investment brought another period of prosperity to the province." Phillips, p. 48.

18. *World*, 5 April 1909.

19. *Western Clarion*, 22 May 1909; *World*, 13 April 1909. The term "skid road" had a different meaning in 1909 than it does today. It referred to the first industrial core of the city, populated by working people, especially migrant timberworkers. The phrase comes from the early roads, made of logs, over which timber was "skidded" to the mills. It was a vibrant community, often rough, but a focal point of working class life and culture.

20. *World*, 5 April 1909; Vancouver Police Court Calendar, Volume 11, 6 April 1909.

21. *World*, 5 April 1909.

22. *Western Wage-Earner,* May 1909.

23. *World,* 6 April 1909.

24. *Western Clarion,* 10 April 1909; *Province* 7 April 1909.

25. *Western Clarion,* 10 April 1909; *IW,* 22 April 1909.

26. Vancouver Trades and Labour Council Minutes, 15 April 1909.

27. *Western Clarion,* 17 April 1909.

28. *World,* 13 April 1909; *Western Clarion,* 17 April 1909.

29. *World,* 19 April 1909; *Daily News-Advertiser,* 20 April 1909.

30. *Province,* 2 May 1909; *IW,* 13 May 1909.

31. *World,* 7 May, 8 May 1909; *IW,* 13 May 1909.

32. *World,* 14 May 1909. *Western Clarion,* 15 May 1909.

33. *Daily News-Advertiser,* 16 May 1909; *World,* 17 May 1909.

34. *World,* 18 May 1909; *Western Wage-Earner,* July 1909; *Western Clarion,* 22 May 1909; *IW,* 24 June 1909.

35. *IW,* 24 June 1909; *Western Wage-Earner,* July 1909; *Western Clarion,* 22 May 1909; *IW,* 24 June 1909.

36. *World,* 19 May 1909; *IW,* 24 June 1909; Police Court Calendar, Volume 11, 19 May 1909.

37. VTLC Minutes, 20 May 1909; *World,* 21 May 1909; *Western Clarion,* 29 May 1909, *World,* 28 May 1909; Police Court Calendar, Volume 11, 28 May 1909.

38. VTLC Minutes, 15 April, 6 May, 20 May 1909.

39. VTLC Minutes, 15 April, 6 May, 20 May 1909; *Western Wage-Earner,* April, May, June 1909; *World,* 17 April 1909; quote from *Western Wage-Earner,* June 1909.

40. Vancouver City Council Minutes, 10 May, 25 May 1909.

41. VTLC Minutes, 3 June 1909; *Western Wage-Earner,* July 1909.

42. VTLC Minutes, 3 June 1909; *Western Wage-Earner,* July 1909.

43. *Western Wage-Earner,* July 1909.

44. That the police were operating on their own initiative is further supported by a comparison of arrests for vagrancy in April and May 1909 and 1910. If the police had been acting on the orders of council, it is reasonable to assume that arrests for vagrancy would have escalated in 1909, as they did during the free speech fight of 1912. This would have been an effective tactic to break up the crowds, but would have required the city council's approval, as it would place a great strain on the jail and city resources. But in fact the number of arrests in 1909 is similar to that of 1908 and is markedly less than that of 1910.

45. *World,* 28 May 1909 *Western Clarion,* 5 June 1909.

46. Foner, *The IWW,* pp. 190-191; Scott, pp. 33-40; *IW,* 3 August, 10 August, 24 August 1911; Victoria *Colonist,* 21 July, 22 July 1911. Scott uses this small fray to attack Foner for "left-wing imperialism." The charge seems rather ill-tempered. Scott is quite right to point out that contrary to Foner, complete free speech was not won. Foner's error comes from the early report in the *Industrial Worker,* a source Scott did not consult. Later *IW* accounts noted that the union was limited to a specific area and that the Salvation Army would be subject to the same restrictions. It is not clear why the IWW in Victoria was not inclined to press for complete free speech, as the organization was to do in the following fight in Vancouver. Perhaps the smaller size of the union and

its organizing constituency made the demand less important; perhaps the smaller size of the city meant the Wobblies could still reach their audience even if sequestered in a specific block. In any event, Victoria IWW members seemed pleased with the restoration of the limited, but equal, form of free speech.

47. *World*, 20 February 1912; *B.C. Federationist*, 20 January 1912; McCormack, p. 106; *Western Clarion*, 27 January 1912.

48. *World*, 10 January, 22 January 1912.

49. *World*, 22 January 1912.

50. Cited in Foner, *The IWW*, p. 206. This refutes McCormack's curious assertion that the battles for free speech were based on a "peculiarly American construction" of justice. McCormack, p. 106.

51. *Province*, 29 January 1912.

52. *World*, 29 January 1912; *Daily News-Advertiser*, 29 January 1912; *World*, 1 February 1912.

53. *Province*, 2 February 1912.

54. *IW*, 22 February 1912; *Province*, 12 February 1912.

55. *World*, 12 February 1912; *Province*, 12 February 1912; Scott, p. 47.

56. *World*, 16 February 1912.

57. *World*, 2 February 1912.

58. *B.C. Federationist*, 5 February 1912.

59. Phillips, *No Power Greater*, p. 55.

60. *B.C. Federationist*, 5 February 1912.

61. *IW*, 1 February 1912.

62. *IW*, 8 February 1912.

63. *IW*, 15 February 1912.

64. *Western Clarion*, 10 February 1912.

65. *Western Clarion*, 3 February 1912. *Western Clarion*, 17 February 1912; *World*, 12 February 1912.

66. *B.C. Federationist*, 5 February 1912.

67. *Province*, 12 February 1912. This raises the question of who appointed Pettipiece to the general staff of the working-class.

68. *Province*, 12 February 1912; *World*, 12 February 1912; *Sun*, 13 February 1912.

69. *Sun*, 13 February 1912.

70. *World*, 16 February 1912.

71. *Province*, 12 February 1912;

72. *Province*, 12 February 1912. Jack Scott has suggested that in fact the VTLC/SPC delegation had asked only for free speech at some future date. Indeed, one of the police commissioners told reporters that this was the case. Scott then suggests that the moderates subsequently realized that this could not be sold to the membership, and then decided to deny that they had asked for so little. While this would strengthen my argument, it seems unlikely. The denial of the VTLC/SPC came immediately after the commisioner's statement; if the delegates knew then that their members would not accept such a vague promise, undoubtedly they knew that before the meeting. And if the delegation had asked for free speech in the future, why didn't it accept the mayor's offer? Furthermore, the delegates had begun to arrange a meeting with Premier McBride before the meeting with the commissioners, precisely in

the event that a suitable compromise could not be reached. Scott is too quick to paint the VTLC/SPC leaders as traitors. They did seek a peace treaty, but not at any cost. They knew beforehand that immediate restoration of limited free speech was the minimal acceptable demand, and they offered that. When it was rejected by Findlay and the police commission, they were prepared to go over his head, and they did so.

73. *World*, 16 February 1912.

74. *World*, 17 February 1912.

75. *Province*, 19 February 1912; *World*, 19 February 1912; *Sun*, 20 February 1912; *World*, 23 February, 24 February 1912.

76. *Sun*, 19 February 1912. *Sun*, 20 February 1912.

77. *B.C. Federationist*, 20 February 1912.

78. *World*, 23 February 1912; *IW*, 7 March 1912.

79. *IW*, 22 February 1912.

80. *World*, 2 March 1912; *Province*, 2 March 1912; *IW*, 29 August 1912.

81. *World*, 9 February, 10 February 1912. McCormack, p. 112, also suggests that the rank and file of the SPC and the IWW may have co-operated more fully with the IWW than their party leaders may have liked.

82. *Province*, 29 May 1912.

83. *Western Clarion*, 23 March 1912.

84. Robin, *Rush for Spoils*, p. 123.

CHAPTER 4

Schisms of Class and Ideology

Why were the leaders of the labour movement so quick to denounce the IWW and syndicalism? The answer lies in a mixture of ideology, economics, and culture. It also requires a careful examination of the assumptions many writers have made about the radicalism of B.C.'s labour movement. In particular, the socialism of the SPC must be re-examined, and the unionism of the VTLC and the B.C. Federation of Labour leaders must be carefully outlined.

Historians have been quick to see the SPC as a revolutionary and radical party. Indeed, the party refused to join the Second International because it believed the organization had let in groups that were not sufficiently red. Ross McCormack has argued that the SPC was the "most radical tendency" on the B.C. left, while Bryan Palmer refers to the "vanguard" position of the party. Ross A. Johnson's dissertation—still the most comprehensive work on the SPC—maintains that it held firm to its impossibilist position of "no compromise, no political trading." This view of the party, however, may be challenged on historical and theoretical grounds.[1]

The SPC was devoted to political action, that is, to using parliamentary democracy to make the revolution. As McCormack notes, the party "considered [the state] the vehicle whereby the means of production would be socialized, and thus, the exploitation of the proletariat would be ended." Committed to a strategy of capturing the state to make the revolution, the SPC held that the "ultimate revolutionary action" consisted of "striking at the ballot box." Johnson points out that it was the party's intention to "work within the Canadian constitutional fabric" and overthrow capitalism by "participating in the democratic process." But in deciding to make its stand in the parliament buildings of the state, the SPC adopted a course that, to the IWW, was contradictory and utopian at best; at worst, it was self-serving and elitist.[2]

The decision to seek state power meant the party had to accept the rules of parliamentary democracy. It had to run candidates, raise money for them, and whip up electoral support. To attract votes, it had to repudiate its proud impossibilism that held reform to be both unlikely and useless. Thus, despite the official party denunciation of reform measures, its 1905 electoral program included planks such as the abolition of election deposits, a law against lobbying, a tax exemption for settlers who improved their lots, and a law to force joint stock companies to publish annual returns. By 1910, party secretary D.A. McKenzie was to insist that the SPC had to become a conventional "political machine" that would fight the "two old parties on their own ground." While such reforms and pragmatic politics may have been of value, they flew in the face of impossibilism and revolution.

Once elected, the socialist MLAs formed a tiny minority in the house. If they were to accomplish anything, they had to make deals with the Tory government of Richard McBride. They were forced to compromise so they could win some reforms and thus prove to their constituents that there was some value in electing SPC candidates. As Johnson puts it, "the exigencies of [SPC] *realpolitik* meant that failure to introduce and vote for legislation that would improve the miners' lot meant losing one's seat in the next election." In order to have any action on their legislative program, the socialist members of the legislature were forced to support the Tory Party and prop up its small majority in the 1904-07 session. The result of this compromise and political trading was "a mild flow of labour legislation principally lacking in teeth."[3]

These reforms were a far cry from a workers' state. They channelled resources away from propaganda and support, towards struggles to hold seats in parliament and to raise the party's percentage of the vote. They may even have helped legitimize the Conservative party, for if Tory governments could bring in the legislation advocated by the SPC, what need had workers for socialism? Instead of being a revolutionary vanguard, the party was essentially reformist. As Allen Seager has observed, "the radical Marxism of the SPC coexisted with its practice of democratic socialism," though social democracy might be a better term. Gerald Friesen has similarly argued that though the rank and file members advocated direct action, the "SPC leaders advocated short-term reforms, sought to avoid outbreaks of violence, and assumed the continued relevance of their political party." If actions do indeed speak louder than words, we must conclude that the socialism of the SPC was not very radical.[4]

In adhering to a doctrine of political action, the SPC laid itself open to a charge of elitism. Electoral politics barred low-paid and migrant workers who were unable to meet property and residency requirements required for the vote, while women and Asians were flatly excluded. When the SPC called for workers to mobilize and use the ballot in the 1909 election, the *Industrial Worker* pointed out acidly that of the five thousand Wobblies in the region, only 75 were eligible to register and vote. Parliamentary socialism cut out significant numbers of workers from the class struggle.[5]

In placing its trust in elections and legislation rather than the action of the working class itself, the SPC's politics implied that workers could not, or should not, make the revolution. The role of the masses was to catapult a body of political leaders into power; these leaders would then institute the revolution and rule in the name of the workers. The party's belief that workers' control would first require a "spell of working class autocracy" suggests that the SPC, like the Bolsheviks, would have held power for the working class. Kingsley and Pettipiece insisted that winning electoral seats was important because "actual experience was a prime necessity for workers, and the sooner they set about acquiring domination in social administration the sooner would their ultimate object be attained." If this sounds like common sense, it hides the fact that only a tiny proportion of the working class could ever hope to attain public office, even in a workers' state. Far from being a call for democracy and workers' control, this sentiment was closer to a call for a kind of socialist managerialism.[6]

This was a very different vision than the IWW's belief in direct action and its faith in the ability of the workers themselves to make the revolution and run society. Actual day-to-day control of industry, not legalistic title to property, was the issue, and Wobblies forcefully asserted that "the freedom of the workers from the slavery of capitalism will never be accomplished by the jealousies, ambitions, and intrigues of politicians—even of politicians of that stripe calling themselves Socialists, and the movement is full of them." In the face of the SPC's faith in voting, the IWW replied that "the liberty of the ballot is the greatest comedy of the century." Fred Moore went so far as to argue that

> the *true* revolutionist is not going to throw paper wads in capitalist voting stalls or beat on his chains with paper just because the parliamentarians say the ballot is a weapon of civilization.... All governments reflect the power of the capitalist state; the revolutionists oppose it, instead of either trying to reform it or capture it to smash it.... To talk of the overthrow of existing institutions by taking part in the modern shell game is childish. The revolution began where the belief in the cause of government ceased.

The *Industrial Worker* related the story of a social democrat who asked the Wobblies why they were not in "sympathy" with the "politicians." "[H]e did all he could in the political field for the worker, but he could not work with the IWW because he was not a wage-worker," he explained. Replied an IWW member, "Exactly; and we can't take part in the political game because we are not politicians!"[7]

It may be argued, as it is in Conlin, that too much has been made of the anarchism of the IWW. But if many Wobblies, including Bill Haywood, saw political action as useful, none considered it sufficient. Haywood carried both an IWW card and a Socialist Party of America card, but he had little faith in electoral activity. He suggested that its prime use might be in having socialist governors in place for the revolution, in the hope that they would be more reluctant to call out the troops. The revolution, however, would be made by the direct action of the workers. Even this mild nod to political action was opposed by B.C. Wobblies, who burned copies of the pamphlet in which Haywood's speech appeared. To those socialists who thought the capitalist state could be captured and used for the working class, Wobblies pointed out that "A wise tailor does not put stitches into rotten cloth." Certainly Haywood did not share the "managerial" vision of many socialists: it was he who suggested that the new society would have "no such thing as the State.... [T]he industries will take the place of what are now existing States."[8] In 1908, the union decisively renounced political action when it purged Daniel DeLeon and his socialist party and deleted a clause from the preamble that called for workers to "come together on the political, as well as the industrial field."

The fight over political and industrial action was more than a debate over tactics. It was also a debate over the ways in which workers developed revolutionary consciousness and the kind of consciousness they were supposed to develop. It was similar to the debate in Russia that prompted Lenin's famous pamphlet, *What is to be Done?* The chief ideologues of the SPC, such as Kingsley and McKenzie, believed that union struggles for wages and conditions could not teach workers the lessons needed to make them into revolutionaries. In their view, labour struggles were little more than the attempt of a seller to get a better price for the product. They held that this was logical and understandable in a capitalist system, but that it was unconnected to the revolutionary struggle and was incapable of turning workers into revolutionaries. True political consciousness would have to be brought to the workers by a trained, educated cadre, and the SPC saw itself as filling this role.

The IWW, on the other hand, believed that the ongoing struggle with the boss provided most of the lessons workers had to learn. People did not become revolutionaries spontaneously, but the conditions of working provided the material necessary for a revolutionary outlook. Organizers did not need to give classes in Marxism; they needed only to make explicit the conclusions workers drew implicitly every day. J.S. Biscay, writing on organizing CN workers in 1911, maintained that

> it was not hard to show them that organization was necessary on the job.... They might not know much about economics, but they do know *what they want.* They all know that we don't want a lot of small unions but *one big union.* They already understand that their interest is opposed to the boss and are ready to fight the boss with any weapon at hand. What more do we want? Is not this practically the substance of solidarity and class consciousness? We can leave the theoretical discussions to phylosophers. What the working class wants is not theory or phylosophy but *action.*[9]

The day-to-day struggle showed workers how to fight and it taught them more profound lessons about the nature of power. Fighting for higher wages and better conditions would soon bring workers into open conflict with capital and the state. This conflict would expose the brute force that lay behind employers' rhetoric about co-operation and common interest to reveal the class nature of the system. When they were confronted with the bayonets of the militia, strikers quickly learned the relation of capital to the state. The chaos and criminality of capitalism were there for all to see. The job of the class-conscious worker and organizer was to help others reach the revolutionary conclusion from the observable data of daily existence, but workers would learn through their own struggles for their own goals that a better world required an end to capitalism and the state. Education was necessary, but it served to dispel the smokescreen put up by capital: it exposed the truth, but it did not create it.

It was obvious to the IWW that the working class could, through its own efforts, go far beyond a pure and simple trade union consciousness. The union itself was proof that workers could create a revolutionary syndicalist vision. What workers would not arrive at through their own effort was the limited political consciousness that held parliamentary activity to be of prime importance. Political action of the type advocated by the SPC was not a logical extension of shop floor activity, for the state never appeared to be a liberator. It might be induced to make some reform, but it was all too apparent that the government would always hold its own interests paramount. Joe Hill satirized the unenlightened worker "Mr. Block," who, after being victimized by the boss and the AFL, decides to vote the socialist ticket, with predictable results:

> Election day he shouted, "A Socialist for Mayor!"
> The Comrade was elected, he happy was for fair.
> But after the election, he got an awful shock:
> A great big Socialistic Bull [cop] did rap him on the block.
> And Comrade Block did sob,
> "I helped him to his job."
> Oh Mr. Block you were born by mistake,
> You take the cake; you make me ache.
> Tie a rock on your block and then jump in the lake,
> Kindly do that for Liberty's sake.[10]

There were differences too between social democrats and syndicalists over the role of the intellectual in the movement. The SPC believed that its theorists and ideologues were of great importance, for they shaped and maintained the revolutionary doctrine and interpreted it for others. While the IWW believed that workers had to be class conscious, it did not rely on intellectuals for education. Wobblies denounced "spittoon philosophers," and made it plain that it was "the obscure Bill Jones on the firing line with stink in his clothes, rebellion in his brain, hope in his heart, determination in his eye and direct action in his gnarled fist" who counted "for the most" in the struggle. Wobblies believed that the emancipation of the working class was truly the job of the working class; it needed no help from the renegades of other classes. One sarcastically reflected on the alleged need for intellectuals in the labour movement:

> It is a mystery how the slaves and serfs of the old times ever organized a rebellion without some wise guy to read unto them the 37th chapter of Karl Marx—in the original German. However, they did the best they could to help themselves. Are you doing the best you can—or merely thinking about what some philosopher said? It may comfort the hungry worker to know that defective nutriment causes gastric irritation, but what's the matter with the ham and eggs?

Haywood observed that "Socialism is so plain, so clear, so simple that when a person becomes an intellectual he doesn't understand socialism." To those who spoke to and about the workers while remaining safely apart from them, the union suggested that "the most effective method of 'studying the working class' is not through a microscope or a monocle, but by squinting along the handle of a Number Two [shovel]." To the SPC leaders, this disregard for the niceties of Marxocology and the belief in direct action were heresy.[11]

The IWW did not represent the "economism" Lenin railed against in *What is to be Done?* In fact, no one represented the straw man presented there. No one believed that revolutionary consciousness sprang from nowhere; the issue was, could the pressure for economic demands be used as a springboard for a revolutionary consciousness? Lenin and the SPC argued that it could not; syndicalists argued that it was the only way for workers to develop a truly revolutionary outlook that would abolish all authority over the working class, including a state ruling in its name.

If the radicalism of the SPC leadership needs careful definition, the position of the VTLC and the B.C. Federation of Labour must also be examined. Unlike many AFL locals, B.C. unions were not opposed to industrial unionism. Indeed, the premier issue of the *Western Wage-Earner* called for increased solidarity and the federation of craft unions. At the 1911 AFL convention, the VTLC sponsored a resolution that called for the body to "go on record as favoring industrial unionism and proceed to organize all employees working for one company into one central body." The motion was defeated, but western delegates to the Canadian Trades and Labor Congress of 1911 managed to pass a resolution calling for industrial unionism. In August 1912, the VTLC voted to endorse industrial unions, and Parm Pettipiece announced that "workers must get wise to the fact that what was needed is bigger unions and less unions." Members of the regular trade unions joined with the IWW in attacking Samuel Gompers during his visit to the city: in a much-quoted passage of his memoirs, the AFL president noted that they had "denounced me in the vilest language I have ever heard."[12] And both the VTLC and the Federation played key roles in the formation of the One Big Union in 1919.

But if the labour bodies were moving to industrial unionism, they objected strongly to the radicalism and tactics of the IWW. Leaders of the VTLC and the B.C. Federation of Labour wanted instead to move their members towards parliamentary socialism. The *Western Wage-Earner* noted in 1909 that "workers who disregard and belittle the value of the franchise are neglecting the only thing of value the workers possess." Later in the year, the VTLC passed unanimously a resolution to confer with the SPC "with regard to taking common action at the forthcoming elections." The work to bring together the two organizations culminated in February 1912 when the B.C. Federation of Labour voted to endorse the Socialist Party of Canada as the political party of the working class. At that time, a symbolic gesture illustrated the alliance clearly—the offices of the SPC were transferred to the new Labor Temple. The move reflected the fact that at least 60 per cent of the SPC membership belonged to trade unions. The *de facto* alliance between the two organizations, despite the SPC's impossibilist rhetoric and theoretical critique of trade unionism, meant that the labour movement would eventually be pulled away from considerations of direct action and syndicalism in favour of social democracy.[13]

Why did labour and socialist leaders reject syndicalism and the IWW? More importantly, why did ideology keep the organizations apart, even in the face of state repression? Ideological differences should not have been that important in the face of a common enemy. But the different ideologies sprang from the different cultures and conditions of those who held them, and this helps explain the lack of solidarity among the left-wing groups in B.C.

In order to document this class fragmentation, 278 names of members of the IWW, the SPC, and the trade union movement were combed from the radical and Vancouver daily press from 1909 to 1914. These names were then researched in city directories for this six-year period. This is not what quantifiers would call a random sampling, and one need not be a skilled cliometrician to point out potential problems with the methodology. But the purpose is not to create a hypothetical "average" member of the organizations. Rather, the investigation is a preliminary attempt to determine if the leadership of the Socialist Party and the trade union movement occupied a markedly different class location than members of the IWW.

Of the 278 names found, 134 (48 per cent) were those of trade unionists, 87 (31 per cent) of IWW members, and 57 (21 per cent) of activists in the Socialist Party. Only one was that of a woman, Minnie Scimmell, of the Cooks and Waiters Union. The trade union names are not a list of union members in Vancouver. They are instead a list of men who were active in the union movement, most commonly those who were elected to represent their unions at the trades and labour council. Along with the business agents included in the survey, they were the officers of the labour movement, the leaders and spokesmen who came together to shape collective policy.

Members of the IWW were somewhat more difficult to find. But the *Industrial Worker*, which started publication in Spokane in 1909, was aimed at informing Wobblies the continent over of strikes, free speech fights, general conditions, and jobs. To fulfill this function, it actively solicited reports and letters from members and delegates, and the names of many Vancouver members are in its pages.

Finding the members of the SPC proved to be the most difficult. The pages of the *Western Clarion* were, in the main, devoted to large philosophical questions, but there are reports of the work and members of the Vancouver local, which can be supplemented by those in the daily press. In addition, the *Clarion* published a remarkable list of campaign contributors in 1912, and names from the list were selectively included in this survey. In an attempt to avoid skewing the statistics by counting nickel and dime supporters of the campaign, only those people who donated two dollars or more in 1912 were used.

The first hint of different compositions of the organizations is the ethnicity of their members inferred from surnames. Admittedly this is difficult to establish. Immigrants often changed their names, or had them changed by customs officials; often the most obvious "ethnic" name hides decades of residency in another country. Nonetheless, a comparison between the IWW, the SPC, and the trade unions is possible. Less than 70 per cent of the IWW members had British surnames. In contrast, over 80 per cent of the SPC names were British, while nearly 90 per cent of trade unionists' were. This suggests that the IWW in fact represented recent immigrants and non-British workers in a way the Socialist Party and the AFL unions in the province would not. The numbers also suggest that the leadership of the trade union movement was almost exclusively British.

The members of the IWW were highly mobile. Fifty-three per cent were never listed in the city directories of 1909 to 1914. Among the SPC, 23 per cent were never enumerated, but only 13.5 per cent of the union delegates fail to show up in the directories. None of the Wobblies was listed for all six years. But nearly 11 per cent of the Socialists were listed in the Vancouver directory every year, while 16 per cent of the trade union members were so listed from 1909 to 1914. Nearly half (42.5 per cent) of the unionists are listed in four or more of the six years. While the same exercise nets a significant 14 per cent of the Socialists, only one of the IWW members (1.2 per cent) was in the directories for four years or more. This strongly suggests that members of the IWW were much more likely to be migratory, while both the SPC and the trade union movement had a sizable contingent of more secure, stable workers.

The addresses of the men are also suggestive. Only one Wobbly is listed as the renter or owner of a house, and he lived there only a single year. The remainder of the IWW members lived in hotels, rooming houses, or as tenants in a house owned by another. Most lived in the downtown core, with addresses such as 15–232 East Pender, or the Waldorf Rooms, at 116 West Hastings. A few lived in better parts of town for a time—Arthur Jenkins, for example, is listed at the Maple Leaf Boarding House at 1327 Granville for one year, but later lived with a carpenter at 200 18th Avenue. Many of the SPC members are also found in the downtown core, but men such as Pettipiece and McVety lived in outlying areas. Pettipiece owned his own home at 2349 St. Catherine's Street, while McVety lived at 1876 West 11th Avenue. Delegates to the VTLC were even less likely to live in the downtown area, and were much more likely to live in single family dwellings. Over 16 per cent of the VTLC delegates studied who lived in Vancouver for four or more years stayed in the same house the entire time. This indicates that a segment of the SPC and an even larger segment of the VTLC were geographically distinct from the IWW. These men were able to move to better parts of the city, away from the railways, the docks, and skid road. They were able to afford better housing, even able to purchase homes, instead of being forced to endure the flophouses, cheap hotels, and boarding houses of the city core. Even representatives of the Builders' Laborers' Union, which organized among much the same constituency as the IWW did, were more likely to live outside the city centre. Of the four delegates from the union who can be identified in the directories, only one lived in the downtown area. The other three lived in their own homes in different parts of the city, two of them for the entire six-year period.

The occupations of the members of the three organizations also show different trends. Not surprisingly, most members of the trade unions were skilled workers: machinists, carpenters, cigar makers, and printers figure largely in the rolls. Of the 24 SPC members whose occupations are known, eight were skilled workers and four were labourers. In fact, it is likely that more SPC members were skilled workers, but the Vancouver group seems heavily weighed towards members of the middle class. The few Wobblies whose occupations are listed are split evenly between skilled and unskilled workers, though one was a clerk and another a prospector. Census figures for 1911 show that labourers earned only 70 per cent of the annual income of carpenters and street railway employees, and about 61 per cent of the income of electricians; transient labourers could expect to make even less.[14] This disparity of income between skilled and unskilled hints at very real splits in the labour movement. Better wages could give workers more leisure time; it could give them luxuries and niceties that resembled those of the city's professionals more than those of the lumber workers. It would allow them to purchase a house in the suburbs of the city, to establish themselves in the community, to fashion a family life: in short, to give them a stake in capitalist society.

Nine of the union delegates and eight of the SPC members listed their occupation for at least one year as that of an official of either organization. Nearly 7 per cent of trades unionists and 14 per cent of Socialists held positions as functionaries whose interests may have been rather different from those of the rank and file. Wilfred Gribble of the SPC, for example, listed his occupation as "lecturer," while Donald McKenzie gave his as secretary of the SPC. Both men were prominent impossibilists. Parm Pettipiece is listed as the general secretary of the VTLC from 1910 to 1912; thereafter, his occupation is editor of the *B.C. Federationist*. This job paid $30 a week, or $5 a day for a six-day week. Though hardly untold wealth, his salary was nearly double that of a railway navvy, and his work, we may presume, was rather more pleasant.[15] These officials form a grouping of "brain workers" who were certainly of the working class, but who occupied a significantly different niche than industrial or migrant workers. These self-educated ex-workers did not have to deal with a capitalist boss. Their daily work gave them ample opportunity to debate theoretical issues and the finer points of revolutionary doctrine; it allowed them to observe the class struggle from a slight distance. It may be that in common with intellectuals everywhere, these leaders were quite willing to stay out of the camps and factories that the IWW organized, and their more refined tastes may have contributed to their dislike of the less skilled workers in the union's constituency. As editors, leaders, and theorists, these men were trained to think of themselves as pursuers of truth, and it would not be surprising if they tended to view their beliefs as the result of more careful research and analysis than those of the IWW members. After all, it was their job to reflect on these matters, and surely that should give their opinions added weight. And if they were right, surely the working class movement should follow their lead.[16]

Even more illuminating is the number of SPC and VTLC members who might be described as *petit bourgeois*. Nearly 11 per cent of the SPC and 7.5 per cent of the VTLC names were men who owned businesses. These ranged from the real estate agent Beamish to W.J. Nagle, a delegate to the VTLC who owned a painting contracting firm. Ernest Chapman and Alexander Fenton, both delegates from the machinists' union, had formed the Central Machine Shop by 1909. Frederick Perry, a secretary of the SPC, ran his own tailor shop, eventually plying his trade in the Labor Temple. John Schagat, a secretary of the Lettish local of the SPC in Vancouver, joined with a boardinghouse owner to start a grocery store on Cordova street in 1911, while E.T. Kingsley was the proprietor of a print shop. Together, the officials and businessmen account for nearly a quarter of the socialist and labour activists. This sizable group contained most of the leaders of the two organizations: Pettipiece, McVety, Midgley, Wilkinson, McKenzie, Kingsley, and others fall into either or both categories. In addition, as Johnson indicates, the SPC had "more full-time politicians in its ranks" than any other political group in the province outside the governing party. This characterization of SPC members as *petit bourgeois* may surprise some, but it corresponds to studies of the SPA and the German Social Democratic Party that show their memberships included large numbers of shopkeepers, professionals, and the like.[17]

As leaders of the SPC and the labour movement, these men attained a certain status in the province. Pettipiece, Hawthornthwaite, McVety, and others had, at times, the ear of the mayor of Vancouver and the premier of the province. But this position was based on their utility. The leaders had to have some following, and they had to be able to control it. They also had to be reasonable and willing to compromise, for compromise is the essence of the modern political system. Failure to play the game by the rules would mean their privileged positions would be revoked: no more audiences with the power brokers, no more consultations. Their influence on the ruling class worked only when it was acknowledged by the ruling class; it would be acknowledged insofar as it did not appear too disruptive. Often the SPC and labour leaders would break away, but those who preferred their higher status learned that a willingness to co-operate offered more than intransigence.

While none of the analytical fragments is conclusive by itself, together they form a pattern that indicates that these men were separated from other skilled workers, but especially from those of the IWW, by ethnicity, occupation, income, culture, and even geography. It is hardly surprising that they actively sought to dissociate themselves from the Wobblies in times of labour peace and struggle, for their class positions, indeed, their very lives, bore little resemblance to those of the migrant workers and unskilled navvies.

This concept of a labour "aristocracy" need not imply, as Henry Pelling suggests, that skilled workers were conservative, or that unskilled, poverty-stricken workers are always more radical. Nor does it mean, as Robert McDonald has written, that "workers expressed class feeling more through moderate labourism than doctrinaire socialism."[18] One would be hard-pressed to describe the Vancouver Trades and Labor Council, the B.C. Federation of Labour, and the Socialist Party of Canada as particularly conservative or labourist. As Eric Hobsbawm observed, the labour aristocrats created working class institutions and a "whole system of the ethics of militancy." They maintained a strong sense of occupational and class identification: "when the pickets were out against the boss, [they] knew what to do."[19] But unlike their counterparts in England, the labour aristocrats in B.C. were pressured from below by a more radical group that truly had nothing to lose—the unskilled workers organized into the IWW.

It could be argued that figures such as Bill Haywood resembled the leaders of the SPC and VTLC more than the rank and file of the IWW. Haywood, St. John, Trautman, and others had held paid positions in other unions; Ralph Chaplin and Ben Williams used their artistic and literary talents to avoid the pick and the shovel. But if their backgrounds resembled those of the SPC and VTLC leaders, their choices and ideas did not. The IWW officials left more comfortable jobs to side with the unskilled and powerless. They insisted on the direct action that empowered all the workers and attacked the political action that supported an elite of politicians. The union they served insisted on rank and file control, and denied them the ability to dictate policy or tactics. IWW "leaders" had no real power save that of example. Subject to instant recall, they had no base if they went against the wishes of the rank and file. The union, and these officials, believed that workers could do without political leaders, and the very limited power of the Haywoods and St. Johns and Chaplins was devoted to creating a world in which there would be no bosses or rulers of any sort. Unlike the SPC, these people worked to make themselves redundant. Furthermore, the ideology of syndicalism was explicitly democratic, as it had to be if it were to offer an alternative to trade unionism and socialism. It stressed that a leadership caste would soon become reformist, even conservative. Thus Wobblies took union democracy very seriously. Members fought to keep the union under the control of the rank and file, and those suspected of "pork-chopping" or "pie-carding"—that is, becoming professional union leaders—were fiercely opposed. The culture of these migrant workers, the conditions of their work, their desire to prevent centralization, all contributed to a healthy suspicion of leaders that reined in would-be bureaucrats. The competition between regions, industrial unions, and the general executive board was also important, for in demanding that their particular group be able to act independently, union members ensured that leaders could not control the organization in the way Samuel Gompers controlled the AFL. Through measures such as salary restrictions, annual conventions, easy access to the press, and constitutional limitations on office-holding and powers, the IWW remained democratic, as leaders were forced by principle and a watch-dog membership to pay attention to the rank and file. If this created problems and divisions, it at least avoided the crushing bureaucracy of the AFL and TLC, and the vanguard structure of the SPC, which rarely held its legislated annual conventions and was in practice led by the small cluster of officials and writers in Vancouver. Finally, whatever may be said about IWW "leaders," the real comparison is between B.C. Wobblies and the SPC and VTLC officials, for these are the two groups that tangled in the province. Here there is no doubt: they led very different lives and bore little resemblance to each other.

The labour leaders were caught between their sense of class identification and their position as a markedly better-off stratum. While their rhetoric remained radical, their actions increasingly reflected their superior income and status. These leaders were not "liberals in a hurry"; it is more accurate to describe them as socialists who could afford to wait. The IWW was convinced that their relative wealth moved them to more conservative positions:

> If you are in the woods and find three men camped, one of
> whom has a good bed roll, one has one blanket, and the last
> has no blanket at all, you don't need to stop and ask who

will tend fire. The blanketless man will likely set fire to a dead tree and before morning the other two will be complaining about sparks in their blankets as the act is "too radical." It is the propertyless worker who must keep the fire of revolt burning, let the sparks fall where they may.[20]

Notes for Chapter 4

1. McCormack, p. 17; Palmer, *Working-Class Experience*, pp. 164-165; R.A. Johnson, "No Compromise—No Political Trading: The Marxian Socialist Tradition in British Columbia." Ph.D. thesis, University of British Columbia, 1975. The notion that the SPC was the most radical group on the B.C. left may reflect a particularly Canadian tradition of statism. Canada's political culture and economic development have had stronger traditions of state intervention than the United States, at least in the popular mythology. Anarchism, hoboes, and the IWW have never had the same impact north of the forty-ninth parallel as they have had south of it. American historiography shows at least a grudging affection for an anti-state sentiment that does not exist to the same degree in the Canadian literature. McCormack as a liberal, Johnson as a social democrat, and Palmer as a Trotskyist, all bring a particular bias for the state that reflects on their analyses of the IWW's syndicalism.

2. McCormack, p. 58; Johnson, pp. 10, 239-240.

3. *WC*, 16 December 1905; Johnson, p. 207. Despite his own evidence to the contrary, Johnson holds to his theory that the SPC remained revolutionary and unwilling to compromise. The expulsion of Hawthornthwaite from the party in 1911 is often offered as proof of the party's continuing radicalism, but the purge was a repudiation of his land speculation, not the tactic of compromise. See Johnson, pp. 239-240 for McKenzie's remark, and p. 207 for the SPC's *realpolitik*. For the SPC's legislative record, see Robin, pp. 93-94; the quote is from p. 94. The point is not that reform is bad; it is that the SPC said one thing and did another. The decision to enter parliamentary politics forced it to compromise and change its actions, if not its rhetoric. That the party soon preferred its reformism to revolution is proof of its intentions and real program.

4. Seager, "Socialists and Workers," p. 35; Gerald Friesen, "'Yours in Revolt': The Socialist Party of Canada and the Western Canadian Labour Movement," *Labour/Le Travailleur* 1, 1976, pp. 139-157. Friesen's comments are about the party in 1919, but I believe they accurately sum up its position in the earlier period, especially since its leadership was virtually the same throughout.

5. *IW*, 8 July 1909.

6. The SPC's belief in the "spell of working class autocracy" is cited in McCormack, p. 59; see Johnson, p. 255, for Kingsley and Pettipiece's comment, taken from the *B.C. Federationist* of 12 October 1912.

7. *IUB*, 17 August 1907; *IW*, 18 March 1909; Fred Moore may be found in the *IUB*, 18 May 1907; *IW*, 13 August 1910.

8. McCormack, p. 105; cited in Dubofsky, pp. 167-168.

9. *IW*, 16 November 1911.

10. *IWW Song Book*. 29th edition. Chicago: IWW, 1956, p. 38.

11. McCormack, p. 112; *IW*, 8 May 1913; *IW*, 2 September 1909; Haywood cited in Dubofsky, p. 168; *IW*, 26 October 1910. Foner, *The IWW*, p. 148, Dubofsky, p. 170, and Brooks, p. 109, give similar evidence. Dubofsky also cites the "Bill Jones" remark, which comes from an IWW review of Brooks's book. Alvin Gouldner has pointed out that intellectuals and workers have interests that often differ. He writes that "the interests of intellectuals, then, dispose them to assign greater importance to purely *political* organizations than trade unions. Intellectuals, then, are structurally motivated to induce workers to oppose working-class 'economism' and to encourage 'politics.'" *Against Fragmentation: The Origins of Marxism and the Sociology of Intellectuals*. Oxford: Oxford University Press, 1985, p. 116. Johnson illustrates the emphasis the SPC put on its theorists throughout his thesis.

12. *Western Wage-Earner*, February 1909; *B.C. Federationist*, 23 December 1911; Phillips, *No Power Greater*, pp. 46-51; McCormack, p. 114; *IW*, 29 August 1912; Samuel Gompers, *Seventy Years of Life and Labor*. 1925. Reprint. New York: Augustus M. Kelley, 1967, pp. 425-426.

13. *Western Wage-Earner*, March 1909, August 1909; *Western Clarion*, 17 February 1912. For the SPC membership figures, see McCormack, p. 56, who suggests the number may have been as high as 90 per cent. Palmer, in *Working-Class Experience*, suggests the numbers were between 40 and 60 per cent, but see the *Western Wage-Earner*, July 1909, which considers 60 per cent a conservative estimate.

14. Figures cited in McDonald, "Working Class Vancouver."

15. VTLC Executive Minutes, 3 January 1912.

16. This is, of course, speculation, but many authors have raised these points about working class intellectuals. This analysis has long been part of the syndicalist tradition. The classical reference is Robert Michels, *Political Parties*, 1915. Reprint. Glencoe: The Free Press, 1948. Alvin Gouldner goes so far as to suggest that Marxism itself is essentially a doctrine for intellectuals, not the working class. See, among other works, his *Against Fragmentation*.

17. Johnson, p. 15.

18. Henry Pelling, "The Concept of Labour Aristocracy," in *Popular Politics and Society in Late Victorian Britain*. London: Macmillan, 1968, pp. 55-57; McDonald, p. 34.

19. Hobsbawm, "Trends in the British Labour Movement Since 1850," in *Labouring Men*. New York: Basic Books, 1964, p. 323. See also Hobsbawm's "Debating the Labour Aristocracy" and "The Aristocracy of Labour Re-considered" in *Worlds of Labour*. Russell Jacoby points out the problems of the early labour aristocracy argument and calls for the addition of Michels's analysis in *Dialectic of Defeat: Contours of Western Marxism*. Cambridge: Cambridge University Press, 1981, pp. 120-6.

20. *IW*, 22 May 1913. Perhaps Max Nomad best captured the essence of this segment of the working class when he wrote, "Like Faust, the

rebellious intellectual and self-taught ex-worker has two souls dwelling in his breast. Taken as a group, he is originally, like the worker, at the bottom of the social ladder. He shares the worker's hatred and resentment against a system that denies him the good things of life. Side by side with the worker he struggles against privilege and thus develops all the heroic qualities which that struggle calls forth. But his interests are not identical with his humbler associates. He has his education, his invisible capital, which, sooner or later, as the struggle progresses, enables him and his social group to rise to a position of comfort within the existing or the 'transitional' system—while the worker is told to expect it only under 'pure socialism', which only his grandchildren may live to see. Along with the flame of revolt, a fire less sacred burns in the heart of the leader—the lust for power and its material rewards. Gradually his personal, group, and class interests prevail with him over those of the laboring masses; and his mind, always ready to rationalize his desires, is forever finding convincing arguments to justify his new course. Having achieved recognition, influence, or power, the apostles of yesterday become apostates, the tribunes turn traitors, and the rebels—renegades.

"To be sure, there have always been leaders who, disregarding their personal and group interests, have found a sublimation for their ambition in glory, consistency, and at times in martyrdom." Max Nomad, *Rebels and Renegades*. New York: Macmillan, 1932, pp. vi-vii.

CHAPTER 5

'Don't Mourn—Organize!'

The logging strikes of 1924 marked the last significant organizing drive of the IWW in British Columbia. The union did not
die, but it never again had the same ability to mobilize thousands
of workers under its banners. In the 1930s, despite the creation of
a separate Canadian administration, the IWW in the province
was little more than a debating society.[1]

To ask why the IWW declined is to ask two different questions.
The first is the larger question of "why is there no socialism in
Canada?" For the IWW was not the only organization that failed
to bring into being the commonwealth of toil. The SPC, the Social
Democratic Party, the One Big Union, the Co-operative Commonwealth Federation, the Communist Party of Canada, even
the New Democratic Party, have all had a form of socialism as
their goal. Between them, every conceivable strategy has been
tried: political action, economic action, underground cells,
swings to the left, swings to the right, boring from within, boring
from without, playing up class struggle, and playing up class collaboration. Despite their "pragmatic" tactics, each socialist
organization has proved as utopian as the IWW.

They failed because working people did not rally to the cause in
sufficient number. The real question then becomes, "why is there
little interest in socialism, or no explicit socialist consciousness,
among the bulk of the working class?" Clearly, it is not because
most people are satisfied with their lot. There is an ongoing and
highly visible opposition to the present state of affairs. Working
people constantly resist capital and the state on and off the job.
Absenteeism at work and at the polls indicates that people are
keenly aware that this society does not exist for their benefit.
Industrial sabotage, ranging from "slacking off" to theft and
destruction of company property, to the creation of computer
viruses and worms, is widespread.[2] Public delight with political
scandal underlines the widespread conviction that politicians act

largely in their own interests, while the re-election of corrupt officials may reflect the cynical feeling that the system itself creates and maintains corruption. There is a rich folklore of class hatred and mistrust that holds all businessmen to be crooked and ruthless; the popularity of the country song "Take This Job and Shove It" is a commentary on how people feel about work. Sexism, racism, and right-wing populism are in part expressions of anger and powerlessness that have been twisted so victims fight with other victims instead of the real enemy. Individual acts of resistance, such as substance "abuse," opposition to gun control and seat belt use, and the like, all point to continuing dissatisfaction. The success of the *Rambo* series of movies and others in that genre, which pit the hero against representatives of modern society, shows that many have a great deal of hostility towards the system that has taken away their ability to act with meaning and power. The problem, however, is that these personal revolts and sympathies exist in isolation and are directed at the wrong target. Working largely on the level of emotion, they are not conscious acts against the real powers-that-be. Until the groundswell of personal opposition becomes aware of its motivation, aware of the real enemy, and unites with others, it helps maintain the system, for it allows the oppressed to let off steam. It is this failure to make explicit the implicit dissatisfaction and protest that is the core of the question, "why is there no socialism?"

Though the above examples are drawn randomly from the later part of the twentieth century, the question has been the staple of socialist thought at least since the days of Marx and Bakunin. Many have tried to answer the question for North America. The lack of a feudal aristocracy, some have argued, meant that capitalists did not have to struggle to replace it and become dominant. Since there had been no struggle for capitalism, workers did not have a heritage of class struggle to use as a model; they were unable to create independently the category of class and apply it. At the same time, capitalism was hugely successful in North America. Rich resources, ample markets, and the drive of a new, expanding economy made for a gross national product that gave North American workers a larger share of the wealth than workers in Europe could expect. In such an economy, social mobility was high, and workers were able to improve their lot substantially. The myth of mobility and Horatio Alger success was as important as the reality, and it tended to shift the blame for poverty onto the poor themselves. Ethnic divisions, gender divisions, racial divisions, each played upon with great skill by employers and politicians, kept workers apart. Finally, it has been suggested that North American workers were essentially pragmatic: in the words of David Shannon, they preferred to settle for the "half loaf" of better wages and reforms than to hold out for the "hope of the whole loaf" offered by revolutionaries.[3]

Many of these arguments have been tested and found wanting. The lack of a capitalist revolt against feudalism has not stopped the working class from creating a number of ideologies and movements that challenged capital. In any case, a population composed largely of immigrants would have some memory of other class struggles. In North America, movements based on ideas of independence, local autonomy, and complete democracy contained a radical critique of capitalism based on a notion of "producers"; this concept was as capable of carrying the working class to unity as any other. The success of capitalism is not steady and universal, even in times of growth. Different sectors of the economy respond at different times, and the entire economy is subject to cycles of depression and inflation that disrupt working people. Women, unskilled workers, and ethnic and racial minorities have not shared in the alleged prosperity. If it is granted that North American workers had greater social mobility than those in Europe, it is not clear how this would hamper some kinds of socialist consciousness. In Vancouver, the greater prosperity of trade unionists did not prevent many of them from supporting the SPC, though it may have been a factor in the rejection of the IWW. High mobility may push people towards socialism, as it may raise expectations more quickly than they can be realized and in turn trigger more demands; an improved standard of living may allow people to fight for more radical demands than bread.

Eric Foner has suggested that the question "why is there no socialism in North America?" is based on a number of false assumptions. It is assumed, for example, that the pressures of capitalism will naturally and inevitably lead workers to develop class consciousness that will be expressed in unions and socialist parties, or, it might be added, a mass syndicalist movement. If such parties or movements do not occur in large size, so the argument goes, there must be some outside force that has prevented them. However neat such metaphysical laws of human development may appear, they are not borne out by history. Slaves did revolt on occasion; more often they did not. Some Germans opposed the Nazis; most did not. Sometimes starving peasants stormed palaces and granaries; more often, they stoically tightened their belts and did what they could to survive. Humans have a capacity for heroism and revolt, but they also have a huge capacity for heroism and enduring suffering. It is not possible to examine certain conditions of oppression and expect "appropriate" forms of active resistance.[4]

Lawrence Goodwyn, in his study of the Populist movement that swept the United States in the 1880s and 1890s, has put forward an argument that may help explain the development of the IWW as well. Goodwyn argues that "insurgent movements are not the product of 'hard times.'" In some sense, for some workers, all times are hard times. Insurgent movements, Goodwyn writes, are the "product of insurgent cultures." That is to say, resistance is not often generated spontaneously: it must be learned and practised. For effective mass protest to flourish, movements must be able to create an independent institution (party, union, co-op, council, or the like) where people can create ways of understanding the world that "run counter to those of prevailing authority." A way to attract masses of people must be found. A level of social analysis that was previously "unsanctioned by the culture" must be achieved. Finally, an institutional means that allows the educated mass movement to express the new ideas in an "autonomous political way" must be found. In short, a movement must form around new ideas; it must recruit; it must educate its members, and it must be able to act to implement its new vision. Huge obstacles appear at each step. Many people will not be recruited; others who are may not take up the new ideas; those who do may not all move into action. Strong traditions of suffering in silence, of doing what one is told, any number of folkways and customs that help the powerless to "get along," must be overcome. Though we may hear that "the squeaky wheel gets the grease," all too often we learn through experience that "the mosquito that buzzes the loudest gets swatted first." It has been said that freedom is not a right, it is a habit that must be learned. Old habits must be unlearned; traditions that say don't make waves, go along to get along, and you can't beat the system, must be challenged. Yet these traditions often are part of who we are. It is hardly surprising that most of us most of the time do not forget the lessons of repression and deference that have been passed down for generations.

Once individuals have learned to rebel, they must combine with others if their protests are to have any effect. This requires people with the energy and time to organize, write, and agitate; it requires money for printing, conferences, meetings.[5] At each step of the way, those who profit from the system will do all they can to stop the growing protest. Some rebels may be imprisoned, harassed, even killed, to be made an example of and to intimidate others. The media will defend the status quo, and will reach many more people than those who oppose the system can ever hope to. Potential rebels may be bought off or rewarded for toeing the line, while leaders are faced with decisions that may lead to compromise and disillusionment. These are a few of the obstacles that face developing insurgent cultures; the obstacles that keep such a culture from becoming a popular movement are even stronger.[6]

The IWW created a new ideology of opposition and refined its analysis and strategies. It worked hard to develop what Goodwyn calls a culture of insurgency through its speaking tours, newspapers, pamphlets, free speech fights, and strikes. The union provided places for radical ideas to be discussed, in the pages of the *Industrial Worker* and in the meeting halls, factories, camps, and streets of North America. The IWW's agitation and battles gave the unskilled and migrant workers a sense of self-worth and a belief in their ability to fight back and change their world. It may be appropriate to view the union's first decade as the creation of a culture of revolution. Certainly Ben Williams thought so in 1916 when he wrote that the "IWW is passing out of the purely propaganda stage and is entering the stage of constructive organization." The year saw a significant increase in IWW strength in the U.S.; the union seemed ready and able to become a powerful insurgent movement. Any chances for success, however, were dashed by the First World War.[7]

John Bodnar has suggested other reasons for the failure of working class radicalism. He makes a distinction between radicalism and militancy, a useful distinction that has fallen out of favour with many leftist historians. It is a distinction between ends and means. Briefly, militancy is a measure of the lengths workers will go to in order to win their demands, while radicalism is a measure of how deeply the demands challenge the existing state of affairs. A fight for higher wages, for example, may be very militant: workers may strike, seize company property, even use violence. But the fight for higher wages is not the same as a battle to abolish capitalism and institute workers' control.

There are many problems with such a distinction. Peasants may clamour for cheaper bread, but if in their fury they storm the palace and demand the king's head, it is difficult to say where militancy stops and radicalism begins. It may be that a radical ideology is made more respectable by clothing it in apparently moderate demands, but the call for higher wages remains, at least implicitly, a demand for the redistribution of wealth. Workers themselves may be unaware of the radical content of their actions. Workers also learn from their experiences, and a strike for moderate demands may turn into a more radical fight that challenges the whole system. Battles take on their own momentum, and success in one place may inspire others in a chain reaction that increases militancy and radicalism. Afterwards, when a settlement must be hammered out, rebels may be willing to back away from objectives that cannot be settled by negotiation, such as a demand for control of the factory; in the face of repression, workers may prudently decide to play down their radicalism.

Nonetheless, the distinction between militancy and radicalism is often useful in analyzing disputes. Bodnar interviewed a number of men and women who had been active in the Congress of Industrial Organizations in the 1930s and 1940s to suggest that though they were prepared to be highly militant, the ends they sought were not radical. What emerges from their testimony is a deep commitment to family and community, and a willingness to use tactics that would better protect them through gaining increased wages, better job security, and the like. Though the CIO has been called a mass-based radical movement, these workers say that they supported the radical organizers because they were effective and increased the chances of securing better settlements. Socialism and the Communist Party as ideology were not of much interest, for they held out only a promise; the rank and file militants preferred a "half loaf" now. Workers had their own priorities, and these did not always mesh neatly with those of left-wing leaders and organizers. As Bodnar points out, workers must be pragmatic, for their world may come crashing down at any moment. The loss of a job, a reduction in pay, the possibility of jail or blacklisting are terrifying prospects that threaten the profound ends of family and personal survival. Working people may not ultimately be satisfied with only a bigger piece of the pie, but they may not be able to risk struggling for the loftier goal of socialism unless it is clear that the two struggles are intertwined and have some chance for success.[8]

It may be that these workers, for reasons mentioned above, have played down their radicalism. On the other hand, it is presumptuous to attribute to these people motives they themselves deny. Nor should it be inferred that workers with families are necessarily inclined to conservatism. This idea, often put out in social science theory, implies that radicalism is the special prerogative of men, and is akin to sowing wild oats. It is essentially a reformulation of the notion that wives and children are hostages to fortune. It has been proven false throughout history. Women have been in the forefront of many battles, as wives, single parents, and independent workers. Family pressures on men and women may cause them to be more cautious; on the other hand, they may impel them to radical and militant stances in order to protect the family. The point being made above is that working people often see their lives in terms of family and community, not class. Class is a less obvious category, and one that is harder to rally around. An analogy with soldiers in war may help focus the argument. Many writers have demonstrated that soldiers act heroically and without self-interest not to save the fatherland or the flag or democracy, but to save the lives of their comrades and friends. It may be that we are most able to be selfless when we fight for loved ones, rather than abstractions.

The reluctance of the working class to endorse a specific program of socialism has often been interpreted by the left as a failure that must be explained. But the supposed failure of workers to wholeheartedly turn to socialism may simply mean that as human beings, working people have their own priorities and aspirations. These may not be the same as those of the professional or amateur revolutionary. Too often the educated socialist activists are intent upon pressing their own picture of utopia, unaware that their vision reflects their own class position, their own needs, their own world-view, more accurately than it reflects those of working people. As the anarchist Giovanni Baldelli put it,

Very few people find the meaning of life in surrender to an absolute. People do not want to fight in order to live, or live in order to fight; they simply want to draw from life some sensual or other pleasure, and to achieve some measure of fulfillment in love, companionship, service, and creative work. For the sake of these they surrender each day some of their time and energies to the demands of a life-negating system, of whose life-negation they are often more aware than the revolutionaries themselves because they often suffer from it more directly. They also usually have enough sense not to believe in miracles, and to perceive that after the Revolution, life-negating demands will still be made upon them, while in the process they may lose whatever they hold dear, and life itself.[9]

Nothing in this argument should be interpreted to mean that the working class is accurately represented by trade union leaders who preach simple reformism and business unionism.[10] The continual waves of radical protest, the birth and rebirth of working class organizations, the daily struggles for control over the job in the workplace, and the rank and file hostility to union leaders, seem proof enough to discredit such a view. But it does mean that the working class has been able to fashion its own agendas and timetables in the face of its victories and defeats. If every action has an opposite reaction, the constant need of capital to control and exploit the working class provokes resistance. The form, content, and strength of that resistance varies, depending on all sorts of variables such as the economy, the resources of workers, the reaction of the state, the development of a culture of resistance, the reactions of the working class leaders, and the chances for success. It may be that workers, like others, learn largely from their own experience. As workers, their own struggles against the boss and for a better world will provide the most telling lessons, and they will be able to create forms of organization based on their desires and history. That workers have seldom agreed with the leading elements of the socialist movement about what was to be done tells as much about the insularity and elitism of many socialists as it does about the alleged backwardness of workers.

The very nature of socialist movements and parties may be a further barrier to workers. Meetings can be time-consuming and dull; conversely, they may turn into arenas for fierce polemical debates. Such debates may exclude most of the audience and reward those who have the time and inclination to master the finer points of rhetoric, economics, history, and language. In either case, meetings take workers away from family and friends, and may seem less important than home life and leisure. Once involved with radical movements, one is rapidly immersed in arguments about ideas such as hegemony, productive and unproductive labour, the relative autonomy of the state, dialectical materialism, relative and absolute surplus value, and the like. These discussions by their very nature attract and reward those of an intellectual bent who believe in the sanctity of theory. For many, who honestly believe they have better things to do, such discussions are numbing. More important, they are irrelevant to their lives and struggles. It may be that expecting all working people to be interested in the socialism of the academy is as fanciful as expecting everyone to be equally interested in the metaphysics of Spinoza. That is to say that as the discussion over socialism becomes more arcane and removed from day-to-day realities, it becomes a matter of personal quirks and interests rather than class interests.[11]

It may also be true that socialism tends to offer immediate rewards only to those who can expect jobs in the party or union, or who may gain prestige and power for their service, or who profit from studying it. It may be that some of the working class opposition to socialism lies in the healthy suspicion that those who are promising utopia may be lying to secure some personal advantage. Certainly all other purported saviours of the people, such as friendly bosses and politicians, are acting in such a fashion; what proof is there that the new champions are much different?

All of this may point to the reason for the failure of a number of socialist and democratic movements in North America. There remains a less general question about the IWW: what were the specific reasons for its decline in the years around World War One?

Two of the most important factors in the decline of the IWW in B.C. were the nature of the province's economy and the workers who were the union's main target. The economy was largely based on resource extraction, railway building, and construction, and it was seasonal. Like all capitalist economies, it was subject to "boom and bust" cycles as well as larger waves of expansion and depression. The migrant workers of the IWW would follow jobs across the continent. With the end of the railway boom and the onset of the pre-war depression, Wobblies and other workers simply left the province to find better conditions. If the union were to maintain a strong presence, it had to organize among the more stable workers in urban areas. Partly because of repression, partly because the IWW found it difficult to create a suitable structure, and partly because organizing efforts were snuffed out by AFL officials, the IWW was unable to make much of a dent among these workers. As a result, the union's members remained scattered in pockets throughout the province.

Being a member of the IWW was dangerous. Even in the allegedly law-abiding Canadian frontier, Wobbly organizers were murdered. In Nelson, two members, one the former president of the local, were shot and killed while staying at a hotel in December 1911. Foul play was suspected in the drowning death of a Wobbly near Victoria in February 1912. One Wobbly was murdered at Tête Jaune Cache in May 1913; another was hacked to death with an axe near Edmonton in July 1914. Wallace Connell, secretary of the Kamloops local during the CN strike and a secretary of a Vancouver local, died in August 1914 from a beating suffered at the hands of the police.[12]

Wobblies, like other workers, were victims of the class warfare practised on the job. The pages of IWW newspapers contain scores of obituaries of members crushed by logs, caught in machinery, killed in blasting accidents, or smashed by falling rock. As migrant workers, Wobblies risked death every time they hopped aboard the freight trains. In October 1910, James Wilson, the former editor of the *Industrial Worker*, was killed while riding the rods; a few weeks later, three Wobblies were killed in one night. A cursory examination of the *Industrial Worker* reveals that eight union members were killed in the ten months from October 1910 to July 1911. In the U.S. in one five-year period, more than 24,000 migrants died while trying to hitch on the trains.[13]

In the United States, the IWW grew substantially from 1916 to 1917, but a similar resurgence did not take place in Canada. Much of this growth was due to the success of the Agricultural Workers' Organization that agitated among the migrant farm workers of the American west. No such organizing could take place in B.C., for the large-scale farms that required many seasonal workers to take in the harvest did not exist in the province. The AWO's ability to recruit members was in part due to the rich war-time contracts for wheat that American farmers had received. Able to make large profits and dependent on ample labour to bring the crops in, farmers were more willing to give in to wage demands. With a string of victories to point to, the IWW was able to offer much to the farm labourers. In addition, American Wobblies had nearly three years of grace that their Canadian counterparts did not have. War-time repression of radicals started in Canada in 1914, but because the U.S. did not enter the war until 1917, the IWW there was not subject to the same restrictions. North of the 49th parallel, Wobblies and others were subject to detention and deportation, and the border was carefully watched. So-called enemy aliens were forced to register with the authorities, and the Royal North West Mounted Police intensified its infiltration of the IWW. In September 1918, a federal order-in-council outlawed the IWW and other left-wing organizations.[14]

When America entered the war, its repression of the IWW started in with a vengeance, and the attacks on the main body of the union hurt the Canadian locals as well. On 5 September 1917, U.S. government agents from the Department of Justice raided IWW offices and the homes of its members across the United States. Literally tons of documents and equipment, ranging from office spittoons to love letters written by Ralph Chaplin to his wife, were seized by the officials. Hundreds of Wobblies were arrested in the raids and charged with a range of offences, including conspiracy to obstruct the war. Tried in four mass trials in Wichita, Sacramento, Chicago, and Omaha, more than 160 IWW members were convicted and sentenced to jail terms ranging from five to twenty years. The fines levied against members and the union as a whole amounted to more than two million dollars.[15]

The raids and imprisonments nearly destroyed the IWW. The huge dragnet put most of the best-known organizers and agitators behind bars, including many who had worked primarily in Canada, such as George Hardy and Sam Scarlett. It also forced those who remained free to devote their efforts to raising funds for bail and legal defenses, instead of organizing. Vigilantes, whipped to a patriotic frenzy, used the war as an excuse to harass, attack, and even lynch Wobblies. The U.S. Department of Labor sponsored the creation of company unions and reform measures in industries such as mining and logging to cool worker unrest. The IWW newspapers were banned, and it became an offence to belong to the union.

The massive state repression effectively silenced the IWW during the war years. After the war, the state kept the pressure on. In the United States, the so-called "Red Scare" of 1919 saw many radicals deported, while in Canada, the Mounties continued to infiltrate the IWW and to turn back its members at the border. The federal police regularly received copies of the *General Office Bulletin*, a confidential newsletter sent only to IWW members that contained detailed financial information and union correspondence. Reports of the 1924 convention sent to the locals turned up on the desk of the B.C. superintendent of the RCMP, and were forwarded to Ottawa. In addition to the material forwarded by agents inside the IWW, clipping files and reports from officers across Canada kept the police well informed.[16]

The creation of the Canadian One Big Union in 1919 also hurt the IWW's attempts to rebuild after the war. Superficially, the two unions resembled each other, for the OBU organized among the same workers and called for industrial unionism. But the OBU was never explicitly syndicalist, and its chief spokesmen rejected the label and the content in favour of a more reformist line. The new union's ideology instead represented the fusion of industrial unionism and parliamentary socialism that many in the Socialist Party of Canada had long advocated. If the OBU contained a significant block of syndicalist rank and file members, its leaders were drawn from the SPC, and these seasoned politicos were usually able to control the radicals. Ernest Winch, for example, an SPC member and head of the OBU's Lumber Workers, beat back several IWW challenges to his authority. Though forced to move somewhat to accommodate the rebels, Winch was able to centralize the union and keep "the reins of authority in his own hands." Many Wobblies looked upon the OBU as a pale imitation of their own organization that played both ends against the middle to sign up unwary workers. A "Wandering Wobbly" claimed that the OBU was "safely in the hands of a very few doctrinaire Canadian and English 'commodity struggle' socialists who seemed to want the workers to think the [OBU was] the same as the IWW and the authorities to think that it was not." "Boomer," writing in the *Industrial Worker*, accused the OBU of lifting parts of the IWW's preamble and its red card "with a view to confuse" potential workers that they were joining a new improved version of the union. "Boomer" maintained that One Big Union organizers told radicals that the new union was the "resurrection" of the IWW and told less radical workers that it was affiliated to the American Federation of Labor. The chief aim of the OBU, he charged, was to sign up "members who are too cold-footed to carry an IWW card and live up to the principles of the IWW." Whatever the merits of the opposing sides, the competition between the OBU and the IWW in B.C. was marked by character assassination and bitterness that weakened both unions.[17]

But the IWW did not disappear. For a time, it even looked as if it would recover. Wobblies in B.C. had helped organize the Lumber Workers' Industrial Union, and they eventually replaced it with an IWW affiliate. Lumber workers in the Ontario OBU transferred to the IWW in 1924, and coal miners in Wayne, Alberta struck under the union's colours in the same year.

These successes, however, were not enough to restore the IWW. Two events in particular prevented the union from recovering. First, the success of the Russian revolution and the Bolsheviks in 1917 gave the world a new model for revolutionary activity. Eager to follow what appeared to be a successful formula, many North American radicals left their organizations to join the Communist parties of Canada and the United States. Believing that the vanguard pointed the way to the workers' victory, Wobblies such as George Hardy, Charles Ashleigh, Sam Scarlett, Earl Browder, and William Foster left the IWW for the CP. As many as two thousand rank and file members may have left the union for the party. Even more important than the relative number of card carriers each organization could claim were the numbers of workers in the 1920s and 1930s who struck in their name. In this period, the Communist parties, not the IWW, garnered the most support. Weakened by the war-time repression, deserted by many of its ablest organizers, the IWW was not able to agitate to the same extent. For good or ill, the momentum had passed to the Communists. By 1924, Wobbly George Williams could sadly observe that "Numerically we are no stronger than eight years ago; in spirit and aggressiveness, we have receded."[18]

The final blow was delivered by the union itself when it split into two factions at its 1924 convention. Any chance for a recovery was ended there. Factionalism had always been a problem for the union. At the 1906 convention, revolutionaries headed by Vincent St. John, John Riordan and Daniel DeLeon purged the conservative and corrupt leadership of C.O. Sherman. In 1908, migrant western workers led by J.H. Walsh and eastern workers led by Ben Williams joined forces with St. John and William Trautman to remove DeLeon and to direct the union away from considerations of electoral activity and towards syndicalism. In 1911, Foster tried to have the union accept his tactic of "boring from within," and was rebuffed. In 1912, 1913, and 1914, the union was divided on the issue of decentralization. Though the debate was confused, and confusing, it was not a fight between bureaucrats and those who wanted no structure at all. The so-called centralists were defending the most democratic union in North America: the executive board stated plainly that it was aware of "the danger that will ever lie in centralized power." Decentralizers sought to give the limited powers of the General Executive Board to the different industrial unions. The argument was one of structure, not democracy: was the IWW to be One Big Union or a federation of autonomous industrial unions?[19] Decentralists called for measures that would weaken the central executive and strengthen the locals. They sought the abolition of the GEB and the position of the General Organizer, a reduction of the per capita dues paid to headquarters, and an end to the annual conventions. This last was objected to because it was costly for western locals to send delegates to the convention, and thus they were often under-represented.

Vancouver Wobs were instrumental in creating the most significant bloc of decentralizers, the Pacific Coast District Organization. Its aim was to create a stronger west coast organization that would help the locals co-ordinate speakers, organizing drives, and the production of literature. At the same time, the PCDO argued for the autonomy of industrial unions and locals. But the issue was not as clear-cut as it may seem. Fred Heslewood, a centralizer, was accused of siphoning off union funds to purchase a house; he in turn charged Walker Smith, editor of the *Industrial Worker* and a prominent decentralizer, of putting his wife on the union payroll illegally and of encouraging decentralization for the purpose of disrupting the union. Some Wobblies saw the squabble as a fight between activists who wanted more cohesion in the organization and "chair warmers" who preferred to fight with each other than against the boss. Others thought that the GEB and Heslewood were acting as a bureaucratic machine. This argument gained strength when the board replaced Smith with Heslewood as the editor of the *Industrial Worker*, for reasons that remain unclear. The issue of sabotage was also raised, for Smith had devoted several columns to techniques and discussions of slowing down work and injuring machinery. Many Wobblies, especially those in the east, preferred to keep a lower profile on the question.

B.C. Wobblies reacted to Smith's firing in different ways. One Vancouver local refused to pay for its bundle orders of the *Industrial Worker*; another continued to pay under protest. Kamloops Wobblies fought for the principle of rank and file control and against the censorship implied by the removal of Smith, but they disagreed forcefully with industrial union autonomy. When Vancouver local 322 refused to pay its *Industrial Worker* back order and began to issue its own dues stamps as a way of asserting its autonomy, Kamloops Wobs united with others in Vancouver to purge the local of its separatists and to vote it back into the IWW.[20]

This murky sectarian battle did no real damage in the short term. Unlike other feuds, however, which had refined the character of the union and then ended, decentralization reappeared in 1924. The debate was again one over local autonomy; again, this issue camouflaged a number of others. Both sides held rank and file democracy to be vital. One of the chief centralizers argued that *power* had to remain in the hands of the rank and file, but *energy* had to be centralized so the union could be more than a collection of autonomous individuals. As he put it, the federation of industrial unions would "not work any more than a machine that is not bolted together." Control of the union, however, had to remain with the membership if the IWW was to avoid becoming a hierarchical vanguard.[21]

Other problems surfaced at the 1924 convention. Members fought over the IWW's relationship with the Communists; those who had accepted federal pardons quarrelled with those who chose to remain in prison. The agricultural workers formed one of the strongest industrial unions, and lumber and construction workers viewed them as a threat to their own independence. Personal jealousies and animosities, empire-building, the incompetence of new officials who had replaced those in prison, and the cynicism of members towards these officials, all played a part in the rancorous debates. The convention ended in a split, with a small faction of decentralizers and lumber workers forming a separate Emergency Program faction, and centralizers and others remaining in the IWW. As Fred Thompson notes in the official IWW history, "most members dropped out the middle." Those that stayed were unable to generate ideas for adapting to new conditions in the post-war world. The heated wrangling suggests that Wobblies were devoting their energy to infighting and intrigue, a sign that the union had lost its drive and focus. Though the 1924 split was not the cause of the union's decline, it made it final and irreparable.[22]

It is commonplace to end histories of the IWW by arguing that though the union was crushed, it left a legacy in the form of the industrial unions of the 1930s, labour militancy, working-class culture, and a commitment to civil liberties. This attempt to snatch victory from the jaws of defeat is understandable; it may even be accurate in some respects.[23]

But such a conclusion does not do justice to the IWW's analysis and ideology. Wobblies put forward a logical and thorough critique of capitalism that went far beyond the reformism of the Progressives or the ideas of the socialist parties. Seeing clearly that the real issue was power in any of its forms, the IWW challenged all those who sought to rule others. Henry Frenette summed it up eloquently in 1911 when he wrote,

> It is the purpose of all authority, whether economic or political, to enslave the wage worker. Wage workers should not in any way support any person in authority or any person seeking authority. Give any person enough property or enough political authority and he will be a despot to the full extent of his power.[24]

As William Preston points out, this radical attack on power opposed a growing consensus created and imposed by capital, and increasingly adopted by the right, the centre, and the left. This consensus held that society had to be ordered by a hierarchy and maintained by authority. With its syndicalist ideology, the

IWW was, and is, a reminder that present society is based on exploitation and inequality. The union is also a reminder that another vision is possible.

The end of the IWW as an effective organization had important implications for the socialist and labour movements. Without the syndicalist critique, the left became dominated by the authoritarianism of the Communist Party and the reformism of social democrats. In time, socialism became practically synonymous with state control and regimentation. This version was easy for its opponents to attack, as it ran counter to the aspirations of women and men for freedom and autonomy. Only in recent years has the left been able to move beyond this barren position to try to create an ideology that is both socialist and democratic. Ironically, this synthesis was forged more than eighty years ago by the IWW. Indeed, it was one more powerful than most of the neo-Marxist programs put forward today. The IWW stated, simply and plainly, that working people had the right and the ability to run their own lives. Its critique of capital, the state, labour bureaucrats, and socialist politicians has lost none of its accuracy or sting —quite the contrary. The IWW attack on capital and the state rings as true today as it did in 1905. If some progress has been made with wages and conditions for many workers, the fundamental question of control has not been addressed. Workers have no more say in their work than before; they exert no more control over the state. Billions of dollars of goods and services are produced by working people who receive only a fraction back. The state still exists for the good of the bosses and the politicians, not the people. We are no more free to run our own lives than the strikers along the Fraser River were in 1912. That the union was crushed by far stronger forces is no comment on its keen vision. Activists are still inspired by the history of the IWW; its songs are still sung by militants across North America. Its dream of workers' control, of a world without bosses or masters, is still a powerful one. If the forces arrayed against it seem stronger than they did eighty years ago, the IWW's message is perhaps more necessary than ever. The union today may be unable to lead the fight, but it continues to show us where the battle lines are drawn.

Notes for Chapter 5

1. John Sidaway, interview with Dorothy Steeves. Angus McInnis Collection, UBCSC, Box 52, File 13.

2. See James B. Schultz, "Computer Virus Alert!" *International Combat Arms* 7:4, July 1919, pp. 19-25, 82-83, for the U.S. Department of Justice's belief that "disgruntled employees" fashion "the most common" computer crimes.

3. David Shannon, *The Socialist Party of America*. Chicago: Quadrangle Books, 1967. See his final chapter for a fuller description of the arguments presented in this paragraph.

4. See Eric Foner, "Why is there no Socialism in the United States?" *History Workshop* 17 (Spring 1984), pp. 57-80. Much of the reasoning of the preceding paragraphs is derived from this important and provoking essay. See also my own review essay, *Our Generation* 20:1 (Fall 1988), pp. 109-18.

5. The IWW recognized the need for people to carry out those functions; it did not believe that special privileges or rights should also be accorded them. It may be that, as Michels wrote, "whoever says organization, says oligarchy," but the IWW and other syndicalists have believed that it is possible to adopt measures that will allow those tasks to be undertaken without creating a vanguard. Instant recall, wages no higher than those of the rank and file, rotations of jobs, and re-integration into the workplace are but a few of these measures.

6. Lawrence Goodwyn, *The Populist Movement*. Oxford: Oxford University Press, 1978. This fascinating analysis of the development of mass movement contains much of value for those interested in the dynamics of social protest. I have butchered the elegant argument here in an attempt to pull out some of its insights that have particular relevance to the IWW.

7. Williams cited in Brissenden, pp. 340-341.

8. John Bodnar, *Workers' World: Kinship, Community, and Protest in an Industrial Society, 1900-1940*. Baltimore: Johns Hopkins Press, 1982. Bercuson made a similar distinction in "Labour Radicalism," and was pilloried for it. Over-anxious radicals are apt to mistake the first month of pregnancy for the ninth, as was remarked of Bakunin, and dislike the suggestion that workers are not always ready to revolt. History appears to counter their position.

9. Giovanni Baldelli, *Social Anarchism*. Chicago: Aldine-Atherton, 1971, p. 9.

10. Selig Perlman, *A Theory of the Labor Movement*. 1928. Reprint. New York: August M. Kelley, 1970, and Michael Kazin, *Barons of Labor: The San Francisco Building Trades and Union Power in the Progressive Era*. Urbana: University of Illinois, 1987, both make such an argument.

11. I would agree with Rosa Luxemburg's argument that "no coarser insult, no baser defamation can be thrown against the workers than the remark 'theoretical controversies are only for intellectuals.'" Indeed, I would go further and assert that theory is much too important to be left to intellectuals. The point is that intellectuals, by inclination, training and vocation, tend to elevate theory to a specialized plane. As people

who work with and produce ideas, it is natural enough that they would stress theory, but the product of their labours is all too often too refined, rarefied, and delicate for everyday use. Socialist theory, when it is the purview of the intellectual, may come to resemble religious doctrine more than anything else, and if this provides employment for a new priesthood, it also mystifies those it has supposedly been created to aid. When doctrinal purity becomes the chief qualification for entrance to the movement, intellectuals, not working people, are the beneficiaries. That so much socialist theory is today produced by and for academics should be cause for alarm on the left, for it suggests that socialism itself has become a project for a new class of intellectuals.

12. *IW*, 4 January 1912; Edmonton *Journal*, 26 December 1911; *IW*, 29 February 1912; *IW*, 13 May 1913; *Solidarity*, 15 August 1914; Edmonton *Journal*, 9 July 1914; *Solidarity*, 7 November 1914.

13. *IW*, 26 October, 8 December 1910; Kornbluh, p. 66; for graphic descriptions of the dangers of riding the rods, see Foster, *Pages from a Worker's Life*, pp. 105-140; Frederick Niven, *Wild Honey*. Toronto: Macmillan, 1927. Jack London's experiences are excerpted in *The Canadian Worker in the Twentieth Century*, Irving Abella and David Millar, eds. Toronto: Oxford University Press, 1978, pp. 11-17.

14. Avery, pp. 66, 73-75; Barbara Roberts, "Shoveling out the 'Mutinous': Political Deportation from Canada before 1936," *Labour/Le Travail* 18 (Fall 1986), pp. 77-110; see also her book, *Whence They Came: Deportation from Canada, 1900-1935*. Ottawa: University of Ottawa Press, 1988; S.W. Horrall, "The Royal North-West Mounted Police and Labour Unrest in Western Canada, 1919," *Canadian Historical Review* 61:22 (June 1980), pp. 169-90.

15. Haywood, pp. 290-326; Chaplin, pp. 219-228; Dubofsky, pp. 423-444. See William Preston, *Aliens and Dissenters: Federal Repression of Radicals, 1903-33*. Cambridge: Harvard University Press, 1963, for detailed accounts of the federal government's activity, undertaken in part at the behest of employers in the lumber and mining industries.

16. RCMP IWW file, letter, R.S. Knight to Commissioner, 25 July, 26 October 1924; assorted reports and clippings throughout.

17. See Peterson, "The One Big Union in International Perspective," for a discussion of the ideology of the OBU, as well as my comments in Chapter 1. Bercuson's *Fools and Wise Men* is the only full-length treatment of the union; it documents some of the hostility between the IWW and the OBU. Dorothy Steeves, in *The Compassionate Rebel*. Vancouver: J.J. Douglas, 1977, pp. 44-61, offers an account of the fights in the Loggers' Union that is sympathetic to Winch and the socialists; the quote on Winch holding the reins of the union may be found on p. 56. "Wandering Wobbly" is cited in Bercuson, p. 184; "Boomer's" analysis is from *IW*, 16 October 1920.

18. Gambs, pp. 75-98, is the most interesting source on the Communist ascendancy in this period. Ralph Chaplin and George Hardy outline the CPUSA's calculated efforts to destroy the IWW, though from opposite perspectives. See the IWW's *General Office Bulletin*, June 1924, for Williams's remark.

19. Canadians who have been watching the battles between the federal

government and the provinces may be able to appreciate this struggle. The quote from the GEB is cited in Brissenden, p. 317.

20. Brissenden, pp. 299-320; Foner, *The IWW*, pp. 144-146; Dubofsky, pp. 260-262; *IW*, 14 August, 21 August 1913; *Solidarity*, 28 February, 25 April, 23 May 1914.

21. *GOB*, June 1924.

22. See Gambs for the best analysis of the 1924 factions. His work is much superior to Dubofsky's in this respect, for Dubofsky is determined to argue that the IWW was not interested in the issue of union democracy. Thompson's remark comes from his official history, p. 151.

23. William Preston points out, in "Shall This Be All?" that it is unlikely that Wobblies would want to take any credit for the CIO; it is also unlikely that militancy gets passed on from generation to generation. One may also wonder about the benefits of present-day labour bureaucrats belting out the half-remembered words to "Solidarity Forever" as they negotiate lousy contracts and abandon unorganized workers. Much of the argument that follows is presented in this article, which remains one of the most insightful pieces ever written on the IWW.

24. *IW*, 28 September 1911.

Bibliography

Manuscripts

Minutes of Vancouver City Council, 1909, 1912. City of Vancouver
    Archives
Vancouver City Directories, 1909-1914. City of Vancouver Archives
Minutes of VTLC, 1909, 1912. City of Vancouver Archives.
IWW Convention Minutes, 1913, 1924. Angus McInnis Collection,
    UBC Special Collections, Box 52, File 13.

Newspapers

B.C. Federationist, Vancouver (1911-1914).
Daily News-Advertiser, Vancouver.
Industrial Union Bulletin, Chicago (1907-1909).
Industrial Worker, Spokane, Seattle (1909-1913).
Province, Vancouver.
Solidarity, Newcastle, Pa., Cleveland, Chicago (1909-1914).
Sun, Vancouver.
Western Clarion, Vancouver (1905-1914).
Western Wage-Earner, Vancouver (1909-1911).
World, Vancouver.
IWW *General Office Bulletin*, Chicago, various years.

Theses and unpublished studies

Derksen, Craig. "The Vancouver Free Speech Fight, January-February
    1912: An Episode in Class Conflict." Undergraduate paper, Simon
    Fraser University, 1983.
Hak, Gordon. "On the Fringes: Capital and Labour in the Forest
    Economies of the Port Alberni and Prince George Districts, British
    Columbia, 1910-1939." Ph.D. dissertation, Simon Fraser University,
    1986.
Hovis, Logan M. "The Origins of 'Modern Mining' in the Western
    Cordillera, 1880-1930." Paper presented at the B.C. Studies

Conference, Victoria, B.C., November 1986.

Johnson, R.A. "No Compromise—No Political Trading: The Marxian Socialist Tradition in British Columbia." Ph.D. dissertation, University of British Columbia, 1975.

Leonard, Frank. "'A Thousand Blunders': The Grand Trunk Pacific Railway Company and Northern British Columbia, 1902-1919." Ph.D. dissertation, York University, 1988.

Mouat, Jeremy. "The Context of Conflict—the WFM in B.C., 1895-1903." University of British Columbia, 1986. Photocopy.

Rajala, Richard. "The Rude Science: Technology and Management in the West Coast Logging Industry, 1890-1930." Paper presented at the B.C. Studies Conference, Victoria, B.C., November 1986.

Sweeny, Robert. "Theory, Method, and Sources: The Search for Historical Logic." Paper presented at the Workshop on Regional History, Victoria, B.C., February 1986.

Books

Abella, Irving, and David Millar, eds. *The Canadian Worker in the Twentieth Century*. Toronto: Oxford University Press, 1978.

Allen, Ralph. *Ordeal by Fire: Canada 1910-1945*. Garden City: Doubleday, 1961.

Avery, Donald. *"Dangerous Foreigners": European Immigrant Workers and Labour Radicalism in Canada, 1896-1932*. 1979. Reprint. Toronto: McClelland and Stewart, 1980.

Babcock, Robert H. *Gompers in Canada: A Study in American Continentalism Before the First World War*. Toronto: University of Toronto Press, 1974.

Baldelli, Giovanni. *Social Anarchism*. Chicago: Aldine-Atherton, 1971.

Bercuson, David J. *Fools and Wise Men: The Rise and Fall of the One Big Union*. Toronto: McGraw-Hill Ryerson, 1978.

Bodnar, John. *Workers' World: Kinship, Community, and Protest in an Industrial Society, 1900-1940*. Baltimore: Johns Hopkins Press, 1982.

Bradwin, Edwin W. *The Bunkhouse Man: A Study of Work and Pay in the Camps of Canada, 1903-1914*. 1928. Reprint. Toronto: University of Toronto Press, 1972.

Braverman, Harry. *Labor and Monopoly Capital: The Degradation of Work in the Twentieth Century*. New York: Monthly Review Press, 1974.

Brissenden, Paul F. *The IWW: A Study in Syndicalism*. 1919. Reprint. 2nd edition. New York: Russell and Russell, 1957.

Brooks, John G. *American Syndicalism: The IWW*. 1913. Reprint. New York: Arno and the New York Times, 1969.

Buhle, Paul. *Marxism in the USA from 1870 to the Present Day*. London: Verso, 1987.

Camp, W.M. *Notes on Track: Construction and Maintenance*. 1903. 2nd revised edition. Chicago: Published by author, 1904.

Cherwinski, W.J.C., and Gregory S. Kealey, eds. *Lectures in Canadian and*

Working Class History. Toronto: Committee on Canadian Labour History and New Hogtown Press, 1985.

Conlin, Joseph R. *Bread and Roses Too: Studies of the Wobblies.* Contributions in American History, no.1. Westport: Greenwood Press, 1969.

Craven, Paul. *"An Impartial Umpire": Industrial Relations and the Canadian State, 1900-1911.* Toronto: University of Toronto Press, 1980.

Drury, Horace B. *Scientific Management: A History and Criticism.* 1922, 3rd edition. Reprint. New York: AMS Press, 1968.

Dubofsky, Melvyn. *We Shall Be All: A History of the Industrial Workers of the World.* New York: Quadrangle, The New York Times Book Company, 1969.

Finkel, Alvin. *Business and Social Reform in the Thirties.* Toronto: James Lorimer & Co., 1979.

Finlay, J.L., and D.N. Sprague. *The Structure of Canadian History.* Second edition. Scarborough: Prentice-Hall Canada, 1984.

Flynn, Elizabeth Gurley. *The Rebel Girl—An Autobiography—My First Life (1906-1926).* New York: International Publishers, revised edition, 1973.

Foner, Philip S. *The History of the Labor Movement in the United States.* Volume 2, *From the AF of L to the Emergence of American Imperialism.* New York: International Publishers, 1964.

——— *The History of the Labor Movement in the United States.* Volume 3, *The Policies and Practices of the American Federation of Labor, 1900-1909.* New York: International Publishers, 1964.

——— *The History of the Labor Movement in the United States.* Volume 4, *The Industrial Workers of the World, 1905-1917.* New York: International Publishers, 1965.

——— *"Fellow Workers and Friends": IWW Free-Speech Fights as Told by Participants.* Westport: Greenwood Press, 1981.

The Founding Convention of the IWW, Proceedings. 1905. Reprint. New York: Merit Publishers, 1969.

Gambs, John S. *The Decline of the IWW.* 1932. Reprint. New York: Russell and Russell, 1966.

Garson, Barbara. *All the Livelong Day: The Meaning and Demeaning of Routine Work.* New York: Doubleday, 1975. Reprint. Middlesex: Penguin Books, 1977.

Ginger, Ray. *The Bending Cross: A Biography of Eugene Victor Debs.* New Brunswick: Rutgers University Press, 1949.

Goldman, Emma. *Living My Life.* New York: Alfred Knopf, 1931. Reprint. New York: Dover, 1970.

Gompers, Samuel. *Seventy Years of Life and Labor.* Reprint. New York: Augustus M. Kelley, 1967.

Goodwyn, Lawrence. *The Populist Moment.* Oxford: Oxford University Press, 1978.

Gordon, David, Richard Edwards, and Michael Reich. *Segmented Work, Divided Workers: The Historical Transformation of Labor in the United States.* Cambridge: Cambridge University Press, 1982.

Gouldner, Alvin. *Against Fragmentation: The Origins of Marxism and the Sociology of Intellectuals.* Oxford: Oxford University Press, 1985.

Granatstein, J.L., Irving M. Abella, David J. Bercuson, Craig Brown, and H. Blair Neatby. *Twentieth Century Canada*. Toronto: McGraw Hill-Ryerson, 1983.

Haywood, William D. *Bill Haywood's Book: The Autobiography of William D. Haywood*. 1929. Reprint. New York: International Publishers, 1977.

Heron, Craig, and Robert Storey, eds. *On the Job: Confronting the Labour Process in Canada*. Kingston and Montreal: McGill Queen's Press, 1986.

Hobsbawm, Eric. *Labouring Men*. New York: Basic Books, 1964.

—— *Worlds of Labour*. London: Weidenfeld and Nicolson, 1984.

Jacoby, Russell. *Dialectic of Defeat: Contours of Western Marxism*. Cambridge: Cambridge University Press, 1981.

Kazin, Michael. *Barons of Labor: The San Francisco Building Trades and Union Power in the Progressive Era*. Urbana: University of Illinois, 1987.

Kealey, Gregory S. *Toronto Workers Respond to Industrial Capitalism, 1867-1892*. Toronto: University of Toronto Press, 1980.

Kornbluh, Joyce L., ed. *Rebel Voices: An IWW Anthology*. 1964. Ann Arbor: University of Michigan Press, 1972.

Lenin, V.I. *Collected Works*. Volume 27. Moscow: Progress Publishers, 1965.

Livingstone, James. *Origins of the Federal Reserve System: Money, Class, and Corporate Capitalism, 1890-1913*. Ithaca: Cornell University Press, 1983.

Logan, H.A. *Trade Unions in Canada: Their Development and Functioning*. Toronto: Macmillan, 1948.

Macpherson, C.B. *The Real World of Democracy*. Toronto: Canadian Broadcasting Corporation, 1965.

Marx, Karl. *Capital*. 3 volumes. Moscow: Progress Publishers, 1954.

McCormack, Ross A. *Reformers, Rebels, and Revolutionaries: The Western Canadian Radical Movement, 1899-1919*. 1977. Reprint. Toronto: University of Toronto Press, 1979.

McKay, Ian. *The Craft Transformed: An Essay on the Carpenters of Halifax, 1885-1985*. Halifax: Holdfast Press, 1985.

McNaught, Kenneth. *The Pelican History of Canada*. Revised edition. Middlesex: Penguin Books, 1976.

Michels, Robert. *Political Parties*. 1915. Reprint. Glencoe: The Free Press, 1948.

Miliband, Ralph. *The State in Capitalist Society: The Analysis of the Western System of Power*. 1969. Reprint. London: Quartet Books, 1973.

Montgomery, David. *Workers' Control in America: Studies in the History of Work, Technology, and Labor Struggles*. 1979. Cambridge: Cambridge University Press, 1984.

—— *The Fall of the House of Labor: The Workplace, the State, and American Labor Activism, 1865-1925*. Cambridge: Cambridge University Press, 1987.

Morton, Desmond, with Terry Copp. *Working People: An Illustrated History of the Canadian Labour Movement*. Revised edition. Ottawa: Deneau, 1984.

Naylor, R.T. *The History of Canadian Business. 1867-1914*. 2 volumes. Toronto: James Lorimer, 1975.

Niven, Frederick. *Wild Honey*. Binghampton: Dodd, Mead, and Company, 1927.

Noble, David. *America by Design: Science, Technology, and the Rise of*

Corporate Capitalism. New York: Alfred A. Knopf, 1977.

Nomad, Max. *Rebels and Renegades*. New York: Macmillan, 1932.

Ormsby, Margaret. *British Columbia: A History*. Toronto: Macmillan, 1958.

Palmer, Bryan D., ed. *The Character of Class Struggle: Essays in Canadian Working-Class History, 1850-1985*. Toronto: McClelland and Stewart, 1986.

—— *A Culture in Conflict: Skilled Workers and Industrial Capitalism in Hamilton, Ontario, 1860-1914*. Montreal: McGill-Queen's University Press, 1979.

—— *Working-Class Experience: The Rise and Re-Constitution of Canadian Labour, 1800-1980*. Toronto: Butterworth and Company, 1983.

Pelling, Henry. *Popular Politics and Society in Late Victorian Britain: Essays*. London: Macmillan, 1968.

Perlman, Selig. *A Theory of the Labor Movement*. 1928. Reprint. New York: August M. Kelley, 1970.

Phillips, Paul. *No Power Greater: A Century of Labour in B.C.* Vancouver: B.C. Federation of Labour and the Boag Foundation, 1967.

Pollard, Harold R. *Developments in Management Thought*. London: William Heinemann, 1974.

Preston, William. *Aliens and Dissenters: Federal Repression of Radicals, 1903-1933*. Cambridge, Ma.: Harvard University Press, 1963.

Renshaw, Patrick. *The Wobblies: The Story of Syndicalism in the United States*. New York: Anchor Books, 1968.

Roberts, Barbara. *Whence They Came: Deportation from Canada, 1900-1935*. Ottawa: University of Ottawa Press, 1988.

Robin, Martin. *The Rush for Spoils: The Company Province, 1871-1932*. Toronto: McClelland and Stewart, 1972.

Schwantes, Carlos. *Radical Heritage: Labor, Socialism, and Reform in Washington and British Columbia, 1885-1917*. Vancouver: Douglas and McIntyre, 1979.

Scott, Jack. *Plunderbund and Proletariat: A History of the IWW in B.C.* Vancouver: New Star Books, 1975.

Shannon, David. *The Socialist Party of America*. Chicago: Quadrangle Books, 1967.

Smith, Gibbs M. *Joe Hill*. 1969. Reprint. Salt Lake City: Peregrine Smith Books, 1984.

Steeves, Dorothy G. *The Compassionate Rebel: Ernest Winch and the Growth of Socialism in Western Canada*. 1960. Reprint. J.J. Douglas, 1977.

Taylor, Frederick W. *Scientific Management*. 1947. Reprint. Westport: Greenwood Press, 1972.

Thompson, E.P. *The Making of the English Working Class*. Revised edition. Middlesex: Penguin Books, 1968.

Thompson, Frederick W., and Patrick Murfin. *The IWW: Its First Seventy Years, 1905-1975*. Chicago: The Industrial Workers of the World, 1976.

Trachtenberg, Allan. *The Incorporation of America: Culture and Society in the Guilded Age*. New York: Hill and Wang, 1982.

Traves, Tom. *The State and Enterprise*. Toronto: University of Toronto Press, 1979.

Tyler, Robert. *Rebels of the Woods: The IWW in the Pacific Northwest*.

Eugene: University of Oregon Books, 1967.

Wiebe, Robert H. *The Search for Order, 1877-1920.* New York: Hill and Wang, 1967.

Wilentz, Sean. *Chants Democratic: New York City and the Rise of the American Working Class, 1788-1850.* New York: Oxford University Press, 1984.

Articles

Bercuson, David J. "Labour Radicalism and the Western Industrial Frontier, 1897-1919." *B.C. Historical Readings,* edited by Peter W. Ward and Robert A.J. McDonald. Vancouver: Douglas and McIntyre, 1981, pp. 452-473.

Bercuson, David J. "Through the Looking Glass of Culture." *Labour/Le Travailleur* 7 (Spring 1981), pp. 95-112.

"Building Railway in Settled Country." *Industrial Canada,* October 1911, pp. 261-263.

Drache, Daniel. "The Formation and Fragmentation of the Canadian Working Class: 1820-1920." *Studies in Political Economy* 15 (Fall 1984), pp. 43 89.

Foner, Eric. "Why is There no Socialism in the United States?" *History Workshop* 17 (Spring 1984), pp. 57-80.

Friesen, Gerald. "'Yours in Revolt': The Socialist Party of Canada and the Western Canadian Labour Movement." *Labour/Le Travailleur* 1, 1976, pp. 139-57.

Heron, Craig. "The Crisis of the Craftsman: Hamilton's Metal Workers in the Early Twentieth Century." *Labour/Le Travailleur* 6 (Autumn 1980), pp. 7-48.

Horrall, S.W. "The Royal North-West Mounted Police and Labour Unrest in Western Canada, 1919." *Canadian Historical Review* 61:22 (June 1980), pp. 169-90.

Kealey, Gregory S. "Labour and Working-Class History in Canada: Prospects in the 1980s." *Labour/Le Travailleur* 7 (Spring 1981), pp. 67-94.

Mann, Eric. "Unions Absent on Sunday are Dead on Monday." *The New York Times,* 1 September 1986, p. 15.

McDonald, Robert A.J. "Working Class Vancouver, 1886-1914— Urbanism and Class in British Columbia." *B.C. Studies* 69-70 (Spring-Summer 1986), pp. 33-69.

McNaught, Kenneth. "E.P. Thompson vs Harold Logan: Writing about Labour and the Left in the 1970s." *Canadian Historical Review* 62:2 (June 1981), pp. 141-168.

Morley, Terry. "Canada and the Romantic Left." *Queen's Quarterly* 86:1 (Spring 1979), pp. 110-119.

Palmer, Bryan D. "Listening to History Rather Than Historians: Reflections on Working Class History." *Studies in Political Economy* 20 (Summer 1986), pp. 47-84.

—— "Modernizing History." *Bulletin of the Committee on Canadian Labour History* 2 (Autumn 1976), pp. 16-24.

—— "Working-Class Canada: Recent Historical Writing." *Queen's Quarterly* 86:4 (Winter 1979/80), pp. 594-616.

Phillips, Paul. "The National Policy and the Development of the Western Canadian Labour Movement." *Prairie Perspectives 2,* edited by A.W. Rasporich and H.C. Klassen. Toronto: Holt, Rinehart, and Winston, 1973, pp. 42-62.

Peterson, Larry. "The One Big Union in International Perspective: Revolutionary Industrial Unionism, 1900-1925." *Labour/Le Travailleur* 7 (Spring 1981), pp. 41-66.

Preston, William. "Shall This Be All? U.S. Historians Versus William D. Haywood, *et al.*" *Labor History* 12:3 (Spring 1971), pp. 435-453.

Roberts, Barbara. "Shoveling Out the 'Mutinous': Political Deportation from Canada before 1936." *Labour/Le Travail* 18 (Fall 1986), pp. 77-110.

Roberts, Wayne. "Toronto Metal Workers and the Second Industrial Revolution, 1889-1914." *Labour/Le Travailleur* 6 (Autumn 1980), pp. 49-72.

Rosenthal, Star. "Union Maids: Organized Women Workers in Vancouver, 1900-1915." *B.C. Studies* 41 (Spring 1979), pp. 36-55.

Seager, Allen. "Socialists and Workers: The Western Canadian Coal Miners, 1900-21." *Labour/Le Travail* 16 (Fall 1985), pp. 23-59.

Schultz, James B., "Computer Virus Alert!" *International Combat News* 7:4 (July 1989), pp. 19-25, 82-83.

Traub, Rainier. "Lenin and Taylor: The Fate of 'Scientific Management' in the (Early) Soviet Union." *Telos* 37 (Fall 1978), pp. 82-92.

Wejr, Patricia, and Howard Smith, compilers. "Fighting for Labour: Four Decades of Work in British Columbia. 1910-1950." *Sound Heritage* 4:4 (1978), pp. 1-78.

Index